Make You Mine

A Novella

Willow Park
Book 1

Bailey Johnson

Cover Design by Megan Parker

Dinkus by Morgan Teal

Editing and Proofreading by Olive Press Publishing

ISBN: 978-1-971195-09-4

The characters and events portrayed in this book are fictitious or are used fictitiously. Any similarity to real persons, living or dead, is purely coincidental and not intended by the author.

All brand names and product names used in this book are trademarks, registered trademarks, or trade names of their respective holders. Bailey Johnsons is not associated with any product or vendor in this book.

To the people waiting for the courage to put it all on the line.
Now's your time babe, take that leap.

You've got this.

Chapter 1

Sibyl

Butterflies fill my stomach. Nerves settle in my chest like a vice grip, winding tighter and tighter. I smooth my hands down my dress, playing with the gathered seam on the skirt.

Why did I agree to this? Hazel said I needed to move on. Victoria said it would be good for me. Currently, I want to throw up all over this Uber. Who does this?

Three weeks ago, I came across a local photographer taking applications for stranger sessions—the cute ones all over social media where they meet for the first time and have a storybook photo session. I've seen a couple of these sessions where the strangers end up in a real relationship afterward. It's adorable, heartwarming, and inspiring. Drunk Sibyl wanted that.

Sober Sibyl hates that drunk Sibyl filled out that questionnaire and matched with someone. I've lived in this county my whole damn life, and the only person I've ever matched with is the asshole I'm trying to get over.

KELLAN

Did you bring your pepper spray?

ME

No. I did not

KELLAN

Sibs… you're meeting a stranger

ME

Several actually.

There's going to be a photographer and her assistant, Kel. What do you think is going to happen?

KELLAN

I don't know. Anything could happen!

ME

🙄 there's a knife in my purse

KELLAN

Atta girl

I roll my eyes at my brother's dramatics. Tucking my phone back into my purse, I watch the foggy landscape roll by. It's a beautiful day for pictures—the kind of setting that's dreamy, yet a little bit moody. If I'd scheduled this shoot for myself, I'd have wanted this type of weather. Willow Park does some of its best work on a moody day like this. I've been here several times, nursing a bottle of wine, or just to clear my head. In fact, Kellan and I spent a lot of time here as kids.

This park has the cutest little pond with an old wooden dock that's maybe six feet long. Willow trees surround the pond, and an old wooden boardwalk winds through them—a little half-mile walking path that takes you around the water.

It's one of my favorite places on earth. Drunk Sibyl was screaming that this was meant to be. Sober Sibyl wants to bury her head in her hands and scream.

I work the reception desk at my brother's auto body shop. I was raised by a single dad with Kellan as my main companion. Makeup, dresses...none of that is my strong suit. I wasn't surprised at all when the girls showed up this morning. Bags and bags of product, hot tools, and clothes strung over their arms.

My little house looks like a fashion grenade went off in it.

I feel...pretty, though.

Hazel lent me a dark blue dress. It's a soft cotton material. The neckline is lower than I'd normally go for, the elastic wrapping around my shoulders, leaving them bare as loose material flows down my arms. The fabric cinches at my wrists. It's flowy and whimsical and perfect for today.

Victoria curled my long, dark brown hair, leaving it all down, the layers framing my pale face. I don't spend enough time outside, or so the girls tell me. Since Halston broke up with me, I've been as adventurous as going to work and staying home. Pretending I'm a contractor because I've watched a few shows on HGTV and bought a giant mess of a house that needs major renovations. Aside from the hardware store, I haven't gone out in weeks—probably months.

Halston talked about proposing, I even found a ring in his sock drawer. I wish I'd known it was for *her*—that *I* was the experiment. He worked that itch out of his system, and now a perky little blonde three towns over is wearing that ring. I tried to tell her. Hell, all the girls tried to tell her he's an asshole. Naturally, I'm the villain in her story. I caused her man to cheat.

Something tells me she doesn't realize we'd had a relationship for over two years. The way she messaged, I think she thought we had a one-night stand, and she could forgive him for that. I wonder if she'd feel the same way if she knew.

Some hearts just don't want to listen. I know mine didn't. I saw the signs. I knew he was stepping out and still, I waited. I desperately wanted him to choose me. All of my friends are married; my entire friend group—minus my brother—is in loving, committed relationships. I wanted to be next.

Now that I'm here, I'm glad he didn't propose. I would have said yes, and we would have been miserable. Halston isn't going to stop cheating. At least I know it'll never be with me again. He can kick rocks for all I care.

The sleek, black sedan rolls up to Willow Park. My Uber driver, Allen, turns to offer a toothy grin.

"Hope he treats you right, Miss. You look real pretty."

Any other time, I might have thought Allen was being a bit creepy. Today, though, I think the old man really means it.

"Thank you, Allen." I add a nice little tip on the app and slip out the door.

"Sibyl! Hi!" Ramona, the photographer, greets me at the edge of the parking lot. I offer my hand to her, and those butterflies in my belly increase tenfold. Guess there's no backing out now. "Your match is already here, he's got a blindfold on, so I'm going to put yours on, and we'll get you guys set up for photos! Do you trust me?"

She holds out a champagne-colored silk scarf with dark gold swirls throughout it. I gulp, giving her my least convincing smile.

"Don't worry, there's no pressure," Ramona assures me. "You don't have to do anything you don't want, and if the vibes are off, we can absolutely call it. I so appreciate you being willing to do this."

"It's no problem." My smile returns, more genuine this time. "I'm just super nervous. I've never done anything like this."

Ramona ties her hair back into a knot on the top of her head, little blonde wisps framing her face. She's wearing a pair of black overalls that look insanely soft, with a chunky knit sweater hanging off her curvy body. She's gorgeous.

"Maybe you should do the session. I can take decent photos," I say, trying to make a joke.

Ramona, to her credit, lets her head fall back in laughter. "Thank you, but no. I stay behind the camera for a reason."

Extending the scarf again, Ramona offers to take my purse. Tying the scarf around my head, she's careful with my hair, which I appreciate. Tori will kill me if it doesn't look flawless in these photos; it took her close to an hour to curl my stubborn, ridiculously thick hair.

Ramona walks me down the dirt path, and I can almost picture it in my head. Tall grasses reach up and tickle the tips of my fingers. Loose pebbles crunch under my feet. When we get closer to the pond, I hear the soft symphony of wildlife. My chest instantly loosens as I breathe it all in, I love this place. Kellan and I used to spend hours here fishing or chasing frogs with his best friend.

It's like coming home.

"Okay." Ramona's voice startles me. "I'm walking you up to your match. Once I get y'all positioned, you'll be facing away from each other. I'm going to snap a photo of you with your blindfolds on, then I'll take them off, and we'll do a countdown."

I nod.

"Great, you're in place," she says, positioning my body exactly where she wants me. Warmth spreads up my back, the heat of his body emanating through my dress. "Are you comfortable holding hands?" she asks.

I shrug, waiting for the stranger to say something, but he must shrug as well. Cool, soft fingers guide my hand backward, settling it into a warm, rough palm. Fingers intertwine with mine, and I barely hold back a gasp as a zing of electricity spreads across my skin.

"Great! Oh my God, you guys look so cute!" Ramona squeals from somewhere to my right. "Okay, coming for the blindfolds!" She gently takes the scarf off my head, my eyes blinking to adjust. The light disperses through the fog, making it feel even brighter.

When my vision clears, I realize that I'm staring at my favorite willow tree. The sight of it makes me smile, forgetting my nerves.

"Okay, great. Just stay in that pose, and I'll grab a couple shots here." The camera clicks a few times. The nerves return with enough force that I forget how to breathe.

"Alright, you two, on the count of three. One, two, three—"

I turn on my heel. Stunned. Green eyes pierce mine, and a headful of thick, dirty-blond hair shifts as he moves. A smile crosses that too-handsome, too-familiar face.

"Are you kidding me?" I squeal. "Eli!"

Chapter 2

Eli

I'm going to kill my boys. My business partner, Taylor, has been on a mission to get me back into the dating scene. He's ramped up his efforts with my five-year-old's newest obsession: finding a mom.

"All my friends have moms, Dad. I need one too."

It's tough explaining life to a five-year-old on a good day. Trying to tell him it's not that simple when there are tears welling up in those big blue eyes is goddamn near impossible.

That's why I'm standing in Willow Park, a blindfold on my face, my special occasion jeans clinging to my legs. I shuffle my feet again, pulling the fabric away from my skin. The jeans are too damn tight, and the shirt is made from some kind of clingy material.

Taylor's wife, Hazel, left him instructions on what to dress me in: my dark-wash Levis and a dark blue t-shirt—one I had never seen before. Hazel bought it in a size too small, but I took it back to the store to exchange it. I know she meant to show off the muscles I've built after years of working construction, but the thing felt like torture. I wasn't about to show up to a stranger photo session wearing a shirt tight enough that you could see my nipples on camera.

I think back to Tucker's excited little face before I left. "Do you think you'll love her, Daddy?"

"I don't know, Bub." I ruffled his curly brown hair.

"Uncle T and I have a bet that you're gonna love her."

I shook my head, giving him my best smile.

The truth is, I haven't had time to date. Between running my construction business and raising Tucker, I've put myself on the back burner. I have everything I need already. Tucker is my whole entire life. I don't need a partner to make me happy—I'm already happy.

When Lara died in a car wreck, I thought a part of me died with her. I've realized over the years that it didn't. I see that part of me, and all the good parts of Lara, in our son.

He has her picture on his nightstand, but Tucker was only one when she died. He doesn't remember her or the accident. All he knows is that she loved him, but she's not here anymore.

He doesn't know that the pillow I keep in my closet still has her satin pillowcase on it. Her scent has long since worn off, but I can't make myself remove it. Can't let her go. Tucker doesn't get to see the bad nights where I collapse in the shower, barely able to breathe.

Raising him alone was never part of my plan. Losing her? It should have destroyed me. The boys wouldn't let it, though, my two best friends from high school rallied beside me. We have a schedule worked out for Tuck, so he's never forgotten. He's never spent a second in daycare, and there is always someone there to pick him up after school. He has a room at both of their houses. My little man might not have a mom, but he has a family who would go to war for him—and that means more to me than they will ever know.

"Okay." Ramona's slightly raspy voice interrupts the crickets and frogs, bringing me back to the situation I've found myself in. "I'm walking you up to your match. Once I get y'all positioned, you'll be facing away from each other. I'm going to snap a photo of you with your blindfolds on, then I'll take them off, and we'll do a countdown."

I feel the warmth of a body press into my back, palms sweaty with anticipation.

"Great, you're in place," she says to my 'date.' "Are you comfortable holding hands?"

I shrug, hoping whoever's behind me will talk. I want to hear her voice—get a feel for what she's thinking at this moment. I feel her shoulders lift against my back instead. I smile to myself—guess neither one of us are big talkers.

"Perfect!" Ramona slides my arm back, heat twisting up it as a soft hand is pressed into mine. I interlace our fingers, listening as Ramona steps away from us. "Oh my God, you guys look so cute!" Ramona squeals. "Okay, coming for the blindfolds!" The black tie wrapped around my head falls free, my eyes taking a moment to adjust to the foggy afternoon.

I can see the pond from here, a metal rowboat sitting next to the wooden dock. I haven't seen that before, and I've been here plenty of times. I used to fish here with my best friend. We'd spend all day out here in the summer, sometimes it felt like we'd never leave.

"Okay, great. Just stay in that pose, and I'll grab a couple shots here."

I block out the noise of the camera clicking, my chest rising on a deep inhale. *This is crazy. What the fuck am I doing here?*

Soft fingers squeeze mine. I don't know if she's trying to

comfort herself or me, but it helps. I squeeze back, a smile lifting the corners of my lips.

"Alright, you two, on the count of three. One, two, three—"

Our hands break apart as we spin around. Long, dark brown curls fill my vision. Pretty brown eyes peer up at me, squinting when she realizes who she's looking at. I can't help the grin that slashes across my face. A laugh bursts out of my chest.

"Are you kidding me?" she squeals, shoving my shoulder hard enough that I have to take a step back. "Eli!"

"Did you know that we knew each other?" I ask Ramona, but I can't keep my eyes off Sibyl.

This has to be a prank, a perfectly planned and executed prank. There's no way Kellan didn't know we were both coming here to do this. Only...now that I think about it...I told him it was a blind date. I never told him I was doing *this*.

"What the hell are you doing here?" Sibyl grins at me. Her eyes are bright and fuck, she looks beautiful. Stunning.

I rarely see Sibyl Massy outside of work or at her brother's. I can't remember the last time I saw her in a dress. And this dress...I give a low whistle.

"Damn, Sibby." I snatch her hand, twirling her around before drawing her into me.

She giggles, her hands coming up to push my chest away. "Stop it, you idiot."

"This has never happened before." Ramona covers the distance between us in three quick strides.

I almost forgot she was here. Completely forgot she has an assistant filming us not ten feet away. I can't take my eyes off Sibyl. I've never looked at her—not like this. She's

Kellan's little sister. I've never thought about her as more than that.

Maybe it's the fog, or the adrenaline. But I'm looking now. The Massys are good-looking people, and Sibyl is no exception. Her pale skin makes her dark hair and deep brown eyes pop.

The dress she's wearing accentuates her insanely small waist, her hips flaring with the right amount of curve. She's all woman now. And she is fucking gorgeous.

"Where's Tucker?" Sibyl looks around me, like I might have a five-year-old hiding behind my legs. "Oh my God." Big round eyes turn back to meet mine. The depth in them takes my breath away. "Kellan has him, I forgot! He said you had a blind date today!"

She dissolves into giggles, bracing a hand on my forearm to keep herself upright. "How the hell did we match?"

I don't have an answer for that. I've known Sibyl her whole damn life. Never in a million years did I think I'd find myself on a date with her.

"On paper, you two are an ideal match." Ramona reinserts herself in the conversation. "How do you two know each other?"

"I'm her brother's friend." I can't stop fucking smiling. This is wild.

"My brother's *best* friend." Sibyl swipes a thumb at the corner of either eye, laughing so hard she's crying.

"Well, this is crazy." Ramona chuckles, shaking her head. "I totally get it, if you guys don't want to go through with the session."

My heart climbs into my throat. My chest grows tighter as the thought sobers me. I glance back at Sibyl, a soft smile on her face.

I don't *want* to back out of the shoot. My heart skips a beat as the thought catches me off guard.

I did my research. I watched the videos Ramona has on social media. The point of a stranger session is to put people who don't know each other in intimate positions—to see how they connect, or don't.

Sibyl lowers her eyes, avoiding my gaze as the answer gets caught in my mouth.

I can't do this session with Kellan's little sister. Can I?

Chapter 3

Sibyl

My heart is racing so fast, I feel dizzy. Eli Logan is standing in front of me, looking just as handsome as ever.

There has never been any denying how fucking hot he is. The girls and I talk about it weekly, at least, and I'm the only single one between the three of us. Hell, the whole town knows Eli Logan is gorgeous. He's also the least-available bachelor in the county.

Between work and his son, Eli doesn't have time to date. He barely has time for family dinners at Kellan's, but he makes them work because of Tucker. I love that about him. I love how hard he works to make sure Tucker has everything he needs.

What I don't love is the way he's looking at me after Ramona asked if we want to call it off. There is literally no one else on the planet I'd rather do this shoot with. I've had a crush on Eli since I was thirteen. Getting to spend the afternoon posing with him? Pretending to be a couple, even though I know nothing will come out of it? It's too good to pass up.

I'm not so sure he feels the same, though. He looks...

uncomfortable. Maybe he's worried about wasting Ramona's time. He's like that—always trying to be considerate. A rare gentleman in this day and age.

"No, we better n—" I start to say.

"It's up to Sibby. I'm down," Eli says at the same time.

My heart drops into my stomach.

"What?" I breathe, turning my wide eyes to look into his.

"I'm good." His gaze softens, one hand reaching up to move a strand of hair off my forehead.

"Okay." The fuzzy feeling is back in my head. The dizziness increases when Eli bends down to whisper in my ear.

"Breathe, you look like you're gonna pass out."

"Asshole." I swat him away, even as a smile splits my lips.

"You in, Sibyl?" Ramona turns hopeful eyes in my direction.

"Yeah." I heave a dramatic sigh. "Let's do it."

"Yay!" Ramona does a little dance, skipping backward to set up the next picture. "Alright, for this one, I just want you guys to look at each other. Yes, just like that."

I can't stop smiling, and Eli gives me a dopey grin of his own. He disregards Ramona's directions, stepping his toes to mine. Flicking my nose, twisting my hair between his fingers. The longer we stand there staring, the more serious his face gets.

His deep green eyes darken, roaming over my face, down my body. I feel exposed in a way I've never felt before.

"Eli, put your left hand on her cheek. Yes!" Ramona cheers as Eli's rough palm slides across my jaw. His thumb strokes my face, and my eyes flutter closed, head leaning into his warmth.

My heart feels like it's going to pound out of my chest—the way it's banging around in there like a jackhammer. I remind myself to breathe, leaving my eyes closed as he leans forward, pressing a kiss to my forehead.

Holy shit. I am not going to survive this photo shoot. There's just no way I leave here without turning into a puddle.

"Oh my God." Ramona's voice reminds me that we're not alone. "You guys are fucking adorable. Shit, sorry about the language."

Eli laughs. Stepping back, he takes his warm hands with him. "I work construction, it's all good."

"I work in my brother's auto body shop. Trust me. I'm used to it."

"Used to it?" Eli snorts. "You're the one with the filthy mouth."

"Shut up." I roll my eyes. Going to shove him again, he grabs both my wrists, twisting me until he's got my back pinned to his chest. I can't stop the giggles. This is teenage Sibyl's fantasy right here—Eli's big arms wrapped around me, his woodsy, manly scent enveloping me. I tip my head back into his shoulder, trying to get a look at his face, at the smile I hope he's wearing.

He didn't smile much for the first couple of years after Lara died. I've come to cherish the ones he does have. I store them up for rainy days when I need a little sunshine. Because that's what an Eli Logan smile feels like. It's warm, safe, and bright.

"Oh my God, yesss." Ramona holds her camera out in front of her, snapping photos as she switches from vertical to horizontal and back again.

Eli leans his face down next to mine, pressing warm skin into my cheek. "You look beautiful."

A shiver runs down my spine. The smile I'm sending to Ramona's camera is probably cheesy as fuck. I feel like a little kid who got everything on her Santa list.

"Okay, turn to look at each other, maybe rest your foreheads together."

I steady my breath, turning into Eli. He stares at me, a soft smile on his face. I smile back, reaching my hand to rest on his cheek, something warm unfurling in my chest when I watch his eyes close, his head leaning into my palm.

I don't know what my face says when he opens his eyes, but I do know what my brain is saying: I am screaming on the inside, begging him to kiss me. *Kiss me just one time, Eli, so that I know what it's like.*

He must hear it too, because before I'm really ready, Eli Logan's mouth is on mine. His lips are softer than I thought possible, pulling mine apart until I'm open to him.

I tremble in his arms, like some ditzy girl who swoons at the slightest touch. That's what I feel like, being held by him. This has to be a dream—that's the only thing that makes sense. That thought, combined with him pulling back, has me pouting—a full-blown, lower-lip-puffed-out pout.

Eli chuckles, and nips said lower lip then tucks his face into my neck, pressing a little kiss to my bare shoulder before he straightens again.

"Jesus." Ramona fans herself, turning at the waist to look at her assistant. The younger girl is red in the face, her wild brown eyes darting between Ramona and us. "Well, should we try the rowboat?"

"I don't know," I tease. "Eli has a habit of tipping them."

"We can do it last, then." Ramona grins at me, completely missing the joke.

"Thanks." Eli leans down, hot breath tickling my ear as he whispers, "Now she thinks I go around tipping boats over."

"Don't you?" I grin.

"That was one time, Sibyl."

I shudder. I've known this man for my entire life—he's been hanging around our house since before I was born. In my twenty-seven years, I've never heard him say my name like *that*. Never seen him look at me like this either. It's intense.

Now I know why the girls all line up to try and get his attention at the bars. Once his sights are set on you, there's no better feeling in the world. I never want it to stop.

"Okay, I want you guys to hold hands and walk toward the willow."

Eli offers me a big, calloused hand, shooting me a wink when I feel my cheeks heat. This is insane. How the hell is this even happening right now? I let him wrap his fingers around mine, stumbling along next to him down the boardwalk.

"Walk much?" he taunts. I throw my hip into his, nearly causing him to lose his balance. Thank God he didn't. We would have ended up in the water.

"Great!" Ramona calls after us. "Just turn there and, I don't know—"

Eli spins me around, the dress fanning out around me before he puts a hand on my back, the other grabbing my thigh, dipping me.

I squeal like a little girl, gripping his bicep in one hand, the other coming up to rest on his face again.

"Hi," I whisper.

Chapter 4

Eli

I'm going to hell.

Twenty-seven years. I've known her for twenty-seven years as Kellan's little sister, and now that I've tasted her, I can't get enough.

Her skin is so fucking soft. Her lips...

The way she tastes?

How the fuck has she been in my life this whole time, and I never knew touching her would feel like this? It's fucking addictive.

She's got the perfect amount of curve to sink my fingers into. Her hair feels like silk, and the way she's looking at me, with her eyes all hazy? I'm not going to fucking survive this.

"Hi," she whispers. Her sweet, quiet voice is like music to my ears.

"Hey, Sibby girl." I slide my hand up her back until it's tangled in her hair. Flexing my arms, I scoop her into my chest. The need to feel her lips on mine again overrides any logic, along with any loyalty to Kellan.

Sibyl arcs into me. Her lips parting, letting me dip my

tongue inside. We're putting on one hell of a show for the photographer, but I can't seem to care.

I don't know if Sibyl's girls know about this shoot, but Taylor does, which means the whole town is going to learn about it. It's going to go viral, and then Kellan is going to kick my ass for licking his sister's tonsils for the world to see.

The thought is sobering enough that I pull away, winking at Sibyl when she gives me a confused look. I don't want to hurt her feelings, but I need a minute to breathe—to think. Sibyl is family. She's a part of us. I can't fuck this up and lose her. We wouldn't survive that loss. I know it.

I get her back on two feet, tugging her hand—testing a theory. How deep is she in this? How much does she trust me? She follows instantly. Compliant. Her body melts into me wherever I touch her. I forget again that we're being filmed as I tuck her into the base of a willow.

I rest one hand next to her head, bending at the waist, pressing a kiss to her neck. My nose runs along her jaw.

She giggles. It's her nervous giggle, I've heard it a few times, catching her out on first dates over the years, watching her flirt with boys who turned out to be assholes. Boys that Kellan and I took way too much pleasure in beating after they broke her heart. I'm not violent by nature, but there's nothing like a nose breaking under your hand when it's justified, and making Sibyl cry automatically made it justified, in our eyes at least.

But I've never paid much attention to the noise, never had it affect me before. Until today, that is, when it goes straight to my dick—the needy bastard doing his best to make an appearance.

"I need to stop touching you," I breathe into her neck.

"Do you want to stop?" Soft brown eyes meet mine, understanding in them.

"Kellan would—"

"I'm not asking about Kel, do *you* want to stop?"

"No, but I should..."

Sibyl ignores me, offering an award-winning smile to the photographer behind us. I don't know how she's doing it —keeping it together, when I'd like to slam my mouth into hers and find out what she's got on under that dress.

It has to be my lack of any recent relationships. That's gotta be the explanation. I haven't been on a date in years, nor have I tangled with anyone in the past year either. I've been too busy to take a night off for a one-night stand—using my hand to relieve the ache when necessary. Right now, that ache is hard to ignore. My cock is keenly aware of just how freely I've been touching Sibyl.

"Whew, you guys sure you're just friends?" Ramona startles me, her face appearing in my line of sight.

"So far." Sibyl winks, her hand squeezing my forearm.

My body draws taut as a bowstring. Does Sibyl want to be more than friends? She's never shown an ounce of interest—at least none that I've seen. But I haven't been looking either. If I hadn't promised Tucker, I wouldn't even be here. I was convinced I wouldn't find anyone else, and I was okay with that. I had Lara, I have Tucker. I don't need anyone else, but maybe...maybe it'd be okay to want more.

I want this right now. Want *her* right now.

Usually, when I see her, she's fussing over Tucker. The two of them are thick as thieves. Always getting into some kind of trouble that I can't actually be mad about, because staying mad at either one of them is impossible.

I clear my throat, trying not to jump to conclusions, trying to shake out the image of Sibyl passed out on my couch last week. Tucker's little arms wrapped around her neck as they slept, with PAW Patrol quietly playing on the TV.

She's been such a staple in our lives. The thought of her as more—as ours—hits me square in the chest. She's already ours. How didn't I notice it? Notice *her*.

"Hey." Sibyl's head cocks to the side, concern written on her face. "You okay?"

The question is generic, but I see the deeper meaning in her eyes. *Is this okay? Are we okay?*

"All good." I slip my hand in hers, wrapping her fingers in mine again. Her cheeks flush, the prettiest shade of pink climbing all the way to the tips of her ears.

"Ramona asked if we wanted to try the boat."

"Sure." I can't stop staring at her. Pretty sure I'd do anything she asked right now. All my common sense went out the window the moment I turned and saw her.

Sibyl leads me toward the boat. Her dress flows around her, the misty light of the afternoon setting her aglow. Ramona sidesteps across from us, trailing along, snapping photos the whole way.

When we get to the silver boat, I snap out of my trance. Offering a hand to Sibyl to help her get in, letting my brain focus on Ramona's instructions, trying to clear some of the lust out.

"You're only going to go about ten feet off the shore. Anymore, and the fog will make you hard to see. Turn to face me broadside, if you would."

I grunt my assent, hopping into the boat before it's too far off the shore. I guide the vessel to the spot she indicated, turning us so she has the shot she wants. Sibyl's watching me—a look I can't discern etched in her face.

"This is a dream, right? I'm dreaming right now?" Sibyl whispers, almost to herself.

"You dream about me often?" I tease, leaning forward until I hear Ramona say, 'Yesss' from the shore.

"More than I should," Sibyl breathes against my lips.

Fire shoots through my chest, straight to my cock. I take her lips then. The photoshoot completely forgotten as I crash my mouth into hers. I sink my fingers into her hair, angling her head so I can kiss her deeper—claim her. I haven't felt anything like this in so long. It's fucking with my head, muddling my thoughts until all I see is her.

Sibyl squeaks. Her body softens when she opens for me, tongue sweeping into my mouth, matching me stroke for stroke. She surges into me the same moment I lean into her.

One second I'm warm, pulling Sibyl into me, and the next I'm flailing, capsizing into the pond as the boat dumps us into cool water.

Instinct has me reaching for Sibyl, my hands gripping the fabric on her hips, bringing her to the surface with me. She's a terrible swimmer. With this dress on, she doesn't have the best odds in the water, even if she could probably touch the bottom on her tiptoes.

We burst through the water, Sibyl sputtering, Ramona and her assistant staring wide-eyed.

Sibyl's eyes narrow at me, her father's temper climbing to the surface when I wrap her legs around my waist. My hand on her back, I press her core into my erection. Her eyes widen, mouth parting on a gasp when she realizes what she's feeling.

"Eli," she hisses.

"This is not my fault." I grin, smoothing wet strands of hair off her face. My hand settles on her jaw.

"So it's my fault, then?"

"You're the one kissing me like we're alone."

"You kissed me first," she scoffs.

"Eli, can you turn just a quarter—yup, perfect!" Ramona directs us from the safety of the shore.

"I'll do it again. If you make me a promise."

"What's the promise?" She lifts her body higher, using my shoulders to drag her core over my jeans.

I nearly groan, tightening my hold on her waist. "Promise me, when we leave here, it won't be the last time I get to kiss you."

Her eyes darken, one cold hand tracing a finger from my temple to my jaw. "You can kiss me whenever you want."

Fire courses through me like I've never felt before. "How am I just now seeing you?" I cup her jaw, turning her head to meet my gaze.

"I've been here the whole time. I've always seen you," she whispers. Her words hit me so hard, she might as well have slapped me in the face.

"Sibyl..."

She shakes her head. "This isn't the place." Her smile is soft—guarded even. "Plus, you promised me a kiss."

"So I did." I lower her head to mine, pulling at her cold lips, I kiss her softly.

Chapter 5

Sibyl

"Towel's in my truck," Eli mumbles when he deposits me on the shore.

I watch him—t-shirt clinging, every inch of him exposed by his tight, wet clothes. Those jeans are doing nothing to conceal the bulge between his legs.

Ramona and her assistant are trying their best to ignore it. If they weren't here, I might have offered to do something about it.

"Well," Ramona huffs. "That was insane, in the best possible way. Are you two..."

"I'm not sure." I shrug.

I'm not sure of anything. Until today, I thought Eli would always see me as a little sister. He's not as mean as Kellan, but Taylor and Eli have always treated me like a sibling—ruffling my hair, teasing me about my terrible choice in men, beating up the guys who broke my heart.

I always knew Eli was out of my reach. Lara was his soulmate. And I was perfectly content to crush on him from afar. Now that I've felt his hands on me? Kissed him? I don't know how I'm supposed to go back to acting like I don't drool over him every time he stops by the shop and leans his veiny forearms on the counter, tan cargo pants hugging his ass just right.

I'm going to have to move.

Out of state, preferably.

As far away from him as possible.

"Sibby." His voice startles me from my thoughts—a towel extended between us. He's shirtless. His bare chest is shining where it's still wet. A dry t-shirt draped over one shoulder. He towels off the other, his bicep flexing in a taunting display.

My God, I could eat this man up, climb him like a tree, and never come back down.

"So." Ramona clears her throat. "It'll be a couple of weeks for the gallery, and I'll probably post the video on socials in a month or so. Does that work for you two?"

"That's fine." My voice squeaks out.

"Thank you, Ramona." Eli extends a hand.

Ramona's cheeks turn pink when she shakes it, eyes dipping down his naked torso. *Me too, girl, me too.*

"Where's your car?" Eli's attention turns back to me. Goosebumps trail down my arms when I see how close he's standing.

"Too—took a ride-share." My teeth chatter.

Eli glances behind him, head cocking to the side. We're on the path tucked away from the parking lot. Ramona and her assistant are nowhere to be seen now. When his gaze comes back to mine, it's hot enough to start a forest fire.

His fingers hook the elastic on the neckline of my dress, and in one swift pull, I'm left standing in my underwear, in the middle of Willow Park. Goosebumps rise over my whole body when cool air touches my wet skin.

A tortured groan comes from Eli, eyes dipping to the bow on my cotton panties.

"Eli!" I slap his shoulder, snapping him out of his trance.

"Shit, sorry." He rubs the towel over my chest and stomach, slipping his t-shirt over my wet hair. I take the towel from him, stepping out of my dress when he crouches down and taps my calf. He straightens, taking the dress with him.

Squeezing as much water from my hair as possible, I follow Eli back to his truck. How I didn't see the big F-250 that says Logan Construction on the side, sitting in the parking lot, I'll never know.

"You didn't bring a car?" He practically rips the truck door open, his brow furrowed, eyes narrowed at me.

"Kel still has it in the shop." I shrug.

I'm used to Eli being gruff—this is who he is. This is the Eli Logan me and everyone else in the world gets. The guy who just played with me, kissed me senseless, the one who has fun? That's Tucker's dad.

"It could have been some creep. I could have been a rapist, and you would have been stuck here, waiting for a ride-share."

I snort, chucking my purse onto the floorboard. "There was a whole ass photographer here. Plus, it was just you."

Green eyes narrow again, his chest bumping into mine as he leans into my space.

"What do you mean, *just* me?"

I gulp, fortifying myself, trying to get my breathing under control. My back arches into the bench seat as I lean away from him, half of me inside the warmth of his truck. His grip is bruising, but I don't care. Eli might lose control, might unravel altogether, but he would never hurt me. Of that, I am absolutely certain.

"I mean, it's you. I'm safe. So it's fine—"

"Sibby," he growls. "You are anything but safe with me right now."

I'm trembling again, the heat from his hand on my bare thigh burns me up from the inside out. It's the most delicious kind of pain, the way he's barely clinging to his control.

"How long before you need to grab Tucker?" My fingers slip into his thick hair—a gasp bursts between my lips when a wandering hand ghosts over my nipple.

"Kel told me not to hurry back," he murmurs into my skin. His lips pulling, teeth teasing, marking me.

"Eli." My voice comes out like a purr.

"Mmm?" Hooded eyes meet my gaze.

"Get in the truck."

Heat flashes through his eyes. Big, calloused hands grip my thighs, hoisting me off the ground. He all but shoves me into the passenger seat, slamming my door closed, the handle stinging my ass when it connects.

I watch Eli stalk around the back, his door swinging open. One hand holding the lever to move the seat back, the other working the button on his wet jeans. When the seat is back as far as possible, he wiggles out of the dark denim, tossing them to the floor of the back seat. I reach a hand back and knock one leg off Tucker's car seat. Poor kid doesn't deserve a wet seat.

"Come here." Eli reaches across the center console, one hand slipping into my hair. I can feel my face flush, the sudden realization of what we're doing—what I'm doing with Eli Logan—hits me hard.

He doesn't pressure me, doesn't yank me over the center console. Instead, his gaze softens, his fingers untangling from my hair to cup my jaw.

"You okay, Baby?"

My insides turn to lava, heat rolling from my head to my toes in waves. "Yeah," I whisper, maneuvering my body to straddle him in the driver's seat.

"How long, exactly, is always?" he whispers, his thumbs rubbing little circles into my skin. His erection presses into my panties. Two thin layers of cotton separate us.

I could play dumb, pretend I don't know the conversation he's circling back to, but I don't.

"Since I was thirteen, and I realized my brother has hot friends."

"Friends?" He narrows his eyes, hands sliding around to cup my backside, slowly dragging me along the hard length in his lap. A moan slips from my lips.

"You," I breathe. "Specifically, you."

"Why didn't you say anything?"

I quirk an eyebrow at him. What sixteen-year-old would entertain their best friend's kid sister? That's not how it works.

"Not back then, now. You've never said—God." He releases my hips, running a hand through his damp hair. "How have I never seen *you*?"

"Lara is your soulmate. How do I compete with that? And when she died..."

I feel him tense beneath me. This is not something Eli talks about with anyone. Lara dying should have wrecked him. The only reason he didn't lie down and give up is that little boy. I cup his face in my hands, my chest aching at all the hurt he's been carrying alone. "You needed friends—family. Not to be told about a silly crush."

"But still." His grip returns to my ass. "It never went away? You've dated—you—"

"It never went away." I turn to look out the window,

feeling more embarrassed now than when we made out in front of strangers. Ha! Our first kiss was for a TikTok. That's wild.

Warm calloused fingers tuck damp hair behind my ear.

"Sibby..."

I shake my head. This is a mistake. It has to be, right? If we were meant to be together, it would have happened by now. He would have noticed me before some random photographer happened to pair us together.

"Sibyl June, look at me."

I shake my head again. My vision clouds as I hold back tears. He's going to tell me that this shouldn't have happened, going to—

He pinches my chin, dragging my gaze to his. "I wish I would have known."

"Why?"

He releases my chin, scrubbing his hands down his face before he sighs. "I take it back." He huffs out a laugh.

"Oh." I lean away from him. "Okay then—" I push on the door, trying to scramble away from him.

"No, wait," he pleads, hands resting on my sides.

I know he'd let me go if I wanted him to. But I don't. He breathes a sigh of relief when I settle back onto his lap. "I've been so caught up in my own life, in the things that I've lost that I wouldn't have been ready before. Not for someone like you, for something that feels like this."

"Like this?" I breathe.

"Like home," he whispers. "Like everything. I kissed you, and I couldn't stop seeing you asleep on my couch, holding Tucker. I just kept thinking...somehow I missed it."

"Missed what?"

"That you're already ours. I just need to make you mine."

Chapter 6

Eli

Sibyl's lips part, and a little gasp slips between them.

"Please don't tease me." Her voice comes out small, tortured. I could kill that asshole Halston for making her question her worth. And box my own ears in for never realizing how she felt about me.

"I mean it." I slide my hand down her jaw, fingers slipping into her hair, curling around the back of her neck. "I need you to be mine."

She shudders with a shaky breath, a tear slipping down her cheek. I brush it away, searching her eyes for an answer.

Sibyl tilts forward, crashing her lips into mine. Her hips rock, grinding into me.

I groan, gripping her at the waist, shoving her down into my lap.

"Make me yours," she breathes into my mouth.

We're both panting, and my brain spins from lack of oxygen.

She presses into me again, and I can't hold myself back any longer. I slip a hand between us, pulling her panties to the side. My fingers grow slick with her arousal. I toy with her entrance, desperate to feel every single part of her.

Sibyl tips her pelvis, her clit grinding into the heel of my palm. The muscles in her legs draw tight.

"Please, Eli."

"You beg so pretty, Sibby."

Red tinges her cheeks, pupils blown wide. Her gaze is hazy with lust.

"So fucking pretty," I murmur, slipping my middle finger inside of her.

"Uh-uh." She shakes her head. "I don't want your fingers."

Her gaze darts to my lap—to the cotton boxers that are doing a shit job at containing me.

"Baby." I crook my finger inside of her, making her gasp. "I'd like nothing more than to bury my cock inside you right now. But I don't have a condom on me, or even in my house, so you can ride my hand, and when I get you back to your house, you can ride my face."

"I have—" she gasps, her head falling back as she grinds into my palm again. "At my house. I have—" She can't get the words out, too focused on finding her pleasure.

"Even better." I lean forward, licking a path up her neck.

My teeth find her pulse point. Sibyl moans as her sharp fingers dig into my skin. My heart pounds in my chest, dick weeping in my boxers. I meant what I said—I want to be inside her right now. I can wait. I can give her this to start.

Sibyl rocks on my hand, her pace growing erratic, desperate.

"That's it," I whisper. "Take what you need."

She whimpers, her head falling back with a cry when I circle her clit with my thumb. I watch, unable to take my eyes off of her as she falls apart, right there, in my lap, in the cab of my truck.

"So fucking beautiful," I murmur.

Sibyl slumps into my chest. But I need more. So much more.

"Eli?"

"Yeah?" My voice cracks, and I have to clear my throat.

"Take me home?"

I glance at her, and the sight of her looking at me through her lashes steals the air right out of my lungs. I swallow hard.

"Yeah, Baby. I'll take you home."

Sibyl's "house" is a short ten-minute drive that somehow feels like an eternity. It's a tiny two-hundred-eighty-square-foot tiny house that resembles a garden shed more than it does a home. She's incredibly proud of the place, though, so who am I to judge? Especially when it takes only three seconds to carry her from the front door to the foot of her bed.

I set her down and step away, drinking her in.

"Do you want a shower?"

I shake my head. "No. I don't want to shower."

Her eyes dart to my boxers—the cotton material tenting nearly at her eye level.

"Okay," she breathes.

Scrambling across the bed, she yanks open her nightstand drawer hard enough that the whole thing clatters to the floor. "Shit." She giggles.

I grin. Rounding the corner, I snag a foil package off the ground, ripping it open with my teeth.

"Holy shit." Sibyl leans back on her bed, her legs parting for me, pussy glistening from our time in the truck.

"Shirt off, I wanna see all of you."

She wriggles out of my t-shirt, unclasping her strapless bra from the front as perfectly pink nipples peak with the chill in the air.

"Fuck me." I drop my boxers to the ground. Then pull a hand down my shaft as I take her in. "Sibyl." I toss the condom wrapper onto her bed, leaning down to kiss my way up her legs. The salty taste of pond water thick on my tongue.

Rearing over her, I hand her the condom. "You sure?"

Sibyl keeps her eyes on me, one hand grabbing the base of my cock, the other rolling the latex from tip to root. She spreads her legs wider, making room for my hips to settle into hers.

"I'll take that as a yes." I notch myself in her entrance, her eyes still holding mine.

Her gaze full of fire and stars—for me. She's looking at me, like this is everything.

I press into her, inch by inch, until I'm seated fully in her warmth.

"Fuck. You're so fucking tight." Her hips shimmy, seeking friction while I'm doing everything in my power not to come before the first thrust. "Baby," I growl at her. "Give me a minute, or I'm not gonna last."

A wicked grin slashes across that pretty face of hers. She's going to be the death of me. I just know it. Giving me a second to breathe, Sibyl traces fingers over the bridge of my nose, down my jaw to the tops of my shoulders. Her nails dig in as she drags them down my back.

"Fuck," I groan, drawing myself out, torturously slow. Any faster and it'll be an embarrassingly short experience for both of us.

She takes it in stride, moving her body in time to mine, her gasps fueling the fire that's spiraling up my spine. Tingles start in my lower back. "I'm so sorry," I breathe into her neck. "I'm going to—"

"Yes, Eli! Yes!" Sybil gasps my name, her inner walls fluttering as her second orgasm blooms like a flower, slowly unfurling its petals. It's soft and sweet and pulls me over the edge with her.

Stars blur my vision as my orgasm crashes through me. A groan vibrates in my chest. I bury my face in the crook of her neck, breathing her in. She smells like Willow Park, familiar and warm.

"Now I want a shower." I wink at her.

Picking her up with me, I carry her down the hall to the bathroom. We step into her shower, which is as tiny as the rest of her house. The two of us are stuffed in like sardines.

I turn the faucet, and Sibyl yelps when cold water hits her skin. I shuffle her, so my body takes the brunt of the spray.

"Where the hell did you come from, Sibby June?" I can't keep my hands off her. My head dips down to pepper kisses on her throat.

"I've been here the whole time." She grins. "Wish I could say I was waiting for you, but I was pretty sure this would only happen in my head."

I can't hold back a cocky smile. "What did we do?" I whisper in her ear. "In your head. Tell me what we did in your head."

A shiver skates down her spine. I spin us, putting her in

the now warm water. Taking in her bright red face, a laugh bursts out of me.

"That good, huh?"

Sibyl licks her lips, looking down at my cock that's growing again, still in the condom.

"Hold that thought." I slip out of the stall and deposit the used condom in the trash. I stand in the doorway of the shower, watching as she arcs into the spray, washing her hair. Sibyl's body is insane.

I knew she'd started going to the gym with Hazel, but part of me thought they were going to walk on treadmills and talk shit about us boys. But Sibby has some muscle. It's attractive as hell.

"You gonna stand there starin' or get your ass in here to join me?" One coffee brown eye peeks at me, the other still closed. I watch her throat work on a swallow as my breath catches for the millionth time today.

"I'll be honest, I'm tempted to keep staring. It feels like a crime that I never realized how fucking gorgeous you are."

Chapter 7

Sybil

"You're being a little too honest."

He scoffs, stepping into the shower, pushing my hands away when they reach for the conditioner. He squeezes a glob into his palm, then works it through the ends of my hair, moving on to the body wash without trying to rinse it out.

Sometimes, I forget that he was married. It's clear, though, that Eli knows how to care for a woman. I'm on cloud nine knowing it's me that he's caring for.

"You've always been a knock-out. I just never saw it as more. Now that I'm looking, I don't think I'll ever stop."

A slow smile spreads across my face. "By all means." I tip my head at him. I'd spread my arms out, maybe even give him a twirl, if this shower wasn't the size of a linen closet.

"Next time..." His hand slips between my legs, fingers ghosting over my clit. "We're going to my house."

"Next time?" I gasp as his fingers explore me again, slipping through my core.

"Yeah, next time. I told you at the park. I'd kiss you in the water, if you promised it wouldn't be the last time."

"Most people tell you not to give it up on the first date. They say that guys'll lose interest." I peer at him through my lashes, holding my breath.

"Not gonna happen. You're stuck with me." His hand moves further back, cleaning my backside, one finger ghosting between my cheeks. I groan, gripping his forearms, my nails biting into his skin. "You like that, Sibby?"

"Mmm." I hum.

"Have you played here before?" He circles around my rim, the tip of his finger pressing in.

"Yes," I breathe. "With toys."

He gives me a feral smirk. "Can I be the first then?"

"Y—yes." I'm panting by the time he turns me around, bending me into the spray, with one strong hand gripping my hip, and the other rubbing circles on my low back.

"Can I fuck you like this? I'll pull out."

"Yes." I gulp. "I'm on the—" I can't form the words. Thoughts evaporate when I feel the head of his cock notch at my entrance. The sensation of feeling him—all of him—is too much.

"You're on birth control?" He stills behind me.

"Yes." I manage, nodding vigorously.

"Such a good girl. Aren't you?" He presses in further, his hand slipping lower on my back, one finger circling my hole again. "You sure? I don't have to."

"I'm good," I mumble. The words barely escape me as I focus on gripping the faucet so I don't fall over. The last thing I need to do is try to explain to my brother and friends how I busted my face after my blind-date photo shoot.

Eli draws out to the tip, slamming back into me as a finger slips inside my ass. I choke on a cry when the fullness catches me off guard.

"You're doing so good, Baby." He times his thrusts,

matching the pace with his hand and cock. Just when I think it's too much, he switches, alternating between both. "Can you touch yourself? I won't let you fall."

"Hrngh." A nonsensical noise escapes me. One hand releases its white-knuckle grip on the faucet to slip between my legs. The first contact with my clit nearly sends me to my knees. Eli's arm bands around my hips, keeping me upright.

"I can't!" I cry, putting my hand back on the faucet.

Pausing behind me, he takes my hand and presses my finger into my clit. Then his arm comes back around my waist. "You can do it. I've got you. You're doing so well. Look how well you take me."

He slides out, slow and torturous, slamming back in to resume the same brutal pace as before. I peer over my shoulder, watching him between my legs, his finger plunging in and out of me. The image is too much—too fucking good. Instinct has me pressing a finger to my clit, setting off the most powerful orgasm I've ever felt.

Thank God he's holding me. I would have absolutely ended up on my face. Eli's pace becomes erratic, our skin slaps together as he pounds into me. He pulls out of both holes, leaving me empty. His hold on my hips tightens as he finishes on my ass. Hot sticky cum coats my cheeks.

My chest heaves as I try to collect myself, resting my face on the cool plastic wall of the shower. I feel like I'm spinning. My brain is fuzzy, fingertips tingling like I'm not getting enough oxygen in. Holy fuck, I have never had sex like this.

The spray of the shower grows tepid on my skin. But I'm still boiling hot.

Eli washes my body again, before he pecks a kiss to my lips and steals the water for himself. I watch him, content to lean against the shower wall, I memorize the way his muscles flex and contract. He's tall—nearly as tall as my brother and dad. Broad shoulders taper down to a cut waist. His abs are not exactly a washboard, but they're there.

I give up fighting the urge to touch him. Letting my hands wander as he washes, his eyes brighten. A heat fills them when they meet mine.

"Come home with me," he whispers.

"Eli..." I warn, shaking my head.

Sleeping with him is one thing. Staying over at his place, with Tucker? That's different. That's dangerous. Permanent.

"If you're worried about Tucker, you can pretend to leave at bedtime. Takes me ten minutes to get him down, and then you can sneak back in. Hide in my room in the morning. He doesn't have to know you stayed if you don't want him to."

"You can't seriously want me to, can you?"

"Of course I can. Tucker loves you." Eli shuts the water off, reaching a hand to grab towels off the rack. One is usually reserved for my hair, but I suppose I can share with him. I step out of the shower, toes curling into my shaggy bathmat.

"Exactly. I don't want to confuse him."

"What's confusing?" He quirks an eyebrow at me.

"You're being obtuse. I haven't seen you date anyone since—" I catch myself. "In a long time. I'm not sure zero to one hundred is what the two of you need."

"I say what we need." He backs me into the counter, caging me with his arms. "And I say, you're exactly what we need. I still can't wrap my head around the fact that I never saw it before."

"Eli—"

"Please, Sibyl. Stay the night with me. I don't—" His gaze darts over my shoulder, glancing back to meet mine. "I don't want to be alone again, not tonight."

I puff a breath out, already knowing I won't say no. "Fine, but I'm pretending to leave. It's too new, and God, what if something happened? I can't lose Tucker because we have a falling out."

"I would never keep him from you. You're his family."

"I know, but he's your biggest fan. If Tucker thought you were avoiding me, he wouldn't push you to see me."

He shoves off the counter, standing to his full height. "You're right. We can wait. He doesn't need to know right away."

"Thank you." I press onto my tiptoes, kissing his cheek before I head back to my room. "I might have an old pair of Kellan's pants in here."

"Thank God." He picks me up, tossing me onto the bed. He bounces over me, fingers digging into my sides as he assaults me with tickles.

"Stop," I squeal, gasping for breath by the time he relents. "You asshole." I smack his shoulder, grinning.

"Let's get home, pretty girl." Eli presses a kiss to my lips, then shoves off the bed, on a mission to help me find something large enough to fit him.

Chapter 8

Eli

"Sibby!" Tucker bursts through the front door on a mission to find his favorite girl. Sibyl watches him at the body shop after school most days. There's even a little desk at Massy Auto Body where she keeps things for their crafts. When he has homework, she gets it done with him. Even on the days when I can get away early, he still asks to go and see his Sibby.

I don't know how I would have survived without the Massys for the last four years. Tucker calls Sibyl's dad Papa, and her brother has always been Uncle Kel. The thought strikes me like lightning—he's never once called her Auntie. Yet he calls both Hazel and her sister, Victoria, Auntie.

I wait in the doorway between the kitchen and the living area, watching my boy get spun around in circles as Sibyl wraps him up in hugs and kisses. "How's my favorite boy?"

"Dad went on a date today." Tucker grins.

"Oh, did he?" One dark eyebrow shoots up her forehead. "Did he tell you about it?"

"Nope, but he's gonna get me a mama. All my friends have mamas." Tucker's head cants to the side, and two little lines crease his forehead as he takes in Sibyl. "You don't have a mama, do you?"

"I don't. Uncle Kel and I grew up with just Papa."

"Weren't you sad not having a mama?"

"Sometimes." Sibyl kneels to get on his level. "Sometimes it was hard to see everyone else with two parents. But Papa loved us like your daddy loves you. It was more than enough for us. We have the best daddies, don't we?"

"Yes!" Tucker pumps his fist into the air.

"I'm making your favorite for supper, Bud." She winks at him, ruffling his hair as she stands.

"Dad! Sibby's making A'sghetti."

"Is she?"

"Mhm!"

"Well, why don't you go put your bag on the hook and wash up so we can eat?"

"Daddy said you're staying for dinner." Tucker says it like a statement, not a question. Sibyl grins at him, starry-eyed.

"Yeah, Buddy. I'm staying." Her gaze swings to mine. There's something more in that statement—more than just supper. She wants to stay, and I want her here.

"Okay, I'll be right back!" Little feet tear out of the kitchen and I take my time to prowl toward her. My hands are itching to touch her. The half an hour it took to extricate Tucker from Kellan was too much time away from her.

"He doesn't call you Auntie," I whisper, my forehead dropping onto hers.

"He does not," she whispers back, brown eyes shimmering up at me.

"Has he ever?"

She shakes her head. A slow smile spreads across her lips. "No, I'm just Sibby."

I slide my hand down her jaw, wishing her hair were down so I could slip my fingers through it again. "There is no *just* when it comes to you."

I press a tender kiss to her lips, jumping back when Tucker crashes down the stairs, heading toward our direction.

"A'sghetti!" he screams, slamming his little body into Sibyl's legs.

She bursts out laughing, scooping him up to burrow her face into his neck. I'm dumbstruck, watching the two of them. I've been so busy, trying to make sure Tucker has everything he needs, I never realized the person he needed most has always been here—patiently tending to our needs.

I'm the fool who never recognized her for what she was.

She's ours.

"DAD, can Sibby read my story tonight?" Tucker grins at me from the table that's now covered in glitter and crayons.

"Oh, kiddo, I should probably head home." Sibyl winces, as if the lie tastes sour in her mouth.

"Please? Just one time? You never babysit me at night anymore."

"Because I have you almost every day." She giggles, shaking her head at his puppy-dog eyes.

"It's up to her." I wink.

"Fine," she sighs, letting Tucker haul her up the stairs.

He chats the whole way with her about the book we've been reading together.

I load the dinner dishes into the dishwasher, then put away the craft supplies Sibyl and Tucker used for their after-supper adventure time—as Tuck called it. By the time I make it up the stairs, Tucker's nearly asleep. His eyes drooping, one hand wrapped around Sibyl's, his other arm tucked under his head.

Sybil's sweet voice flows in a steady cadence, like a song. I can understand why it lulled him to sleep. His little fingers loosen on her arm, and Sibyl's gaze moves from the book to Tucker's face. She leans forward, pressing a kiss to his cheek, wiggling out of his grip, to set the book on the nightstand. A smile splits her lips when she catches me watching.

"Hey," she whispers.

"Hey," I murmur into her lips, pressing mine to them in a chaste kiss. "C'mon." I tug her hand, pulling her down the hall with me.

As soon as the bedroom door is closed, I haul her into me, devouring her mouth in a hungry kiss. My hands work to get her bun down, fingers slipping through the silky strands.

A sigh brushes my lips as she melts into me. I back her up toward the bed, stopping for a second to remove my shirt, before I'm back to kissing her.

We topple over as the back of her knees hit the bed. A giggle comes from her sweet lips as I work to get her skinny jeans off.

"Shh," I warn. "I might actually die if we get interrupted."

Her giggle is quieter this time, eyes hungry beneath me.

"Shit." I hop out of my jeans, making my way to lock the

door, in case Tucker decides to get up and ask for water. She watches me stalk toward her, teeth sinking into her pouty lower lip as she peels off her shirt and bra. Her jeans and panties following with a slow, tantalizing display.

My eyes draw down to her mouth before I rip another condom open with my teeth and climb onto the bed next to her. Covering my cock with the latex, I jerk my head toward it. "I wanna watch you ride me."

Her eyes widen, a slow smile crossing her face. She climbs on top of me, straddling my lap. Hovering above me, she shifts forward to press a kiss to my chest, then sinks down, taking my length in one swift go.

We groan at the same time, adjusting to the feel of each other as our breath syncs. Hands on my chest, Sibyl lifts, swirling her hips before she drops back down. I nearly burst right then, hanging on to her hips for dear life.

Sibyl slams herself onto me, taking me like I was made for her. She's barely even blinking while I feel as if I'm rearranging her insides. She settles on a rhythm, swirling and rocking her hips. I let my hands wander, touching every inch of skin I can reach.

I can't take my eyes off her chest, watching her bounce above me. I curl myself up, capturing a nipple with my teeth. A muffled cry spills from her lips, her hand covering her mouth. Her eyes glaze over with lust as I work her nipple over. Moving to the next one, I give it the same treatment.

Muffled moans make it hard for me to concentrate on holding myself back. Sibyl reaches for my hand, pressing the pad of my finger into her clit. She covers her mouth again, her head dropping back as her inner walls pulse around me, drawing my release out with hers.

I watch her face, her eyes closed, lips parted in ecstasy. It's the most beautiful thing I've ever seen.

And just like that, one thought, and guilt barrels through me like a freight train.

I used to say the same thing about Lara. She was the most beautiful woman I'd ever met. I could watch her come apart for hours and never grow tired of it.

Never wanted to be anywhere else.

And now I'm here—in her house. In her bed. With someone else. Someone who is not my wife.

Panic swells inside of me. My grip tightens painfully on her hips.

"Eli, you're—oh." Pain morphs into worry when Sibyl looks at me. "Oh God," she whispers, her tone watery.

"Sibyl," I try to reassure her, but my voice sounds as panicked as I feel.

I don't know how to manage the way I'm feeling. Don't know how to separate the past from the present. I've fucked people in the last four years, but I've never done this. Never made love to someone whom I could also fall in love with. Someone who could be more. Who could replace Lara.

It feels like cheating. It feels...

Sibyl slips off of me, rolling away from me, shoulders shaking. I know she's crying. But I can't make myself go to her. Instead, I end up on the other side of the room, yanking my jeans on, desperate to get out of this situation—to forget that any of this happened. That I let myself feel this again. I already had my person. I already got my happily ever after. You aren't supposed to have those twice. I'm not supposed to have these feelings for someone other than Lara.

"I'm so sorry," Sibyl whispers, slipping into her clothes as tears track down her cheeks.

This is wrong, all of it is wrong. I should hold her. I should tell her it's okay. I can make this be okay.

I should do a lot of things, but I don't. Because what I do is the absolute worst option.

I look the second-best thing that's ever happened to me in the eyes and tell her to leave.

Chapter 9

Sibyl

I CRIED A LOT THAT NIGHT. THE ONE WHERE ELI looked at me like I just broke his heart, like we'd done something so unforgivable, he hated himself.

He said he wanted me. Said he wanted to make me his, and then he looked at me like I broke something.

I scrubbed myself raw in the shower that night. I'd never felt dirtier in my entire life. Eli isn't married, he's a widower, but he still feels like he is. I could see the betrayal clearly on his face.

It's been three weeks, and I haven't seen him since. The gallery from Ramona sits unopened in my email. Her questions about an update go unanswered. The girls and Kellan are pissed at me for refusing to share even the tiniest of details with them about that day.

They assumed it was so bad I couldn't talk about it. Kellan has demanded a name for retribution. They don't know it was the best and simultaneously worst day of my life.

We've been avoiding each other, or rather, I spend hours of my day staring at the shop door, willing him to come in, only to be constantly disappointed when he doesn't.

I don't know how he could have been clearer—between the look on his face and the way he told me to go. I thought he wanted me, but I guess he didn't want me enough.

HAZEL

OK what is going on with you and Ellie?

Ellie

E L I

SHIT!

ME

wdym?

HAZEL

Don't play stupid with me

What the hell is going on?

Tucker said he hasn't seen you in weeks.

ME

He hasn't needed me.

HAZEL

Tucker?

Are you kidding me? That kid adores you and he misses you

ME

Eli hasn't asked 

HAZEL

Then march your hot ass over there and tell him you demand some time with his kid

ME

Not sure that's how it works

HAZEL

Babe...this is weird af.

Even Tay asked what was up with you two.

Another text flashes across my screen. A group chat between Ramona, Eli, and me.

RAMONA

Got your video done and I can't not share! I hope you guys love it. Thank you again for coming out for that session! I'll send you the link once it's posted!!

I groan, sinking into my desk chair. Kellan has started getting suspicious as well. Guess that's what happens when you get tangled up with someone who's basically family. I set my phone down, ignoring the vibration as someone calls me. It's 50/50 on who it is. It could be Eli, calling to smooth things over, to make a plan for the people we love, witnessing us make utter fools of ourselves. My money is on Hazel, though. She doesn't like to be ignored.

Heaving a sigh. Once it stops ringing I return to the text thread from earlier. I sent my phone number on my resume, and Miss Allura Jones sent me a text not thirty minutes later. I would have felt more comfortable doing this over email or even the phone. But here I am, begging for a job interview—over text.

ME

Hello Miss Jones

I am writing to let you know I will be passing through your area tomorrow.

I won't be passing through. I'm making the trip specifically for this.

ME

If you're still looking for someone to fill the front desk position, I would be happy to come in and chat.

I sign my name at the end of the text, something that feels a bit like a crime, if I'm being honest.

I am not surprised when Allura Jones texts me back right away, asking to see me at eleven. I check my watch, counting the hours on my fingers. Juniper Hills is nine hours away. If I want to make the drive and be somewhat coherent for an interview at eleven a.m., I'm going to have to leave now.

"Dad." I call into the house, which is attached to the shop. Massy Auto Body is Dad's baby. Kellan only took it over in the last year or two.

"What's up, Sugar Plum?" My dad rounds the corner, a pair of blue overalls tight over his beer belly, gray hair growing in a ring around the sides of his head—the top completely bald.

"I need to take off. Can you man the desk for the rest of the day? And tomorrow?"

"Sure thing. Everything okay?"

"Totally." I force a smile.

"Well." Dad shuffles past me, plopping into my expensive office chair. I grimace when he leans the backrest as far back as it'll go. Things do not stay nice for long in the Massy household. "You can tell me the truth about it when you get back." He winks. "Or you and I can go for a drive."

I shudder.

When I was in high school, and something bothered me, I would clam up and get real quiet. Dad said he always knew when something was wrong because my spark was dull. So he'd get me in the car, and drive around town...in silence. He wouldn't say a peep. Five minutes of that and I'd crack under the pressure, word vomiting all my troubles until I either felt better or cried it out.

It's a non-issue, though. By the time I get back from interviewing, everyone is going to know anyway.

"I'll tell you everything. Not tomorrow, but the next day."

"Alright, Sugar." He raises a brow when I grab my keys off the pegboard behind the desk.

"Kellan put it outside." I shrug.

Moving a car from the shop is our universal sign that it's been fixed and is ready for pickup. Considering I'm the client, I skip the bill and head straight for my candy-apple-red Mercury Mountaineer that's chilling in the parking lot.

God, I've missed her. Eve has been my ride since I bought her straight out of high school. She's a great little SUV. Most people wouldn't be able to drive their first cars around, but it helps that my brother is both a talented mechanic and body man. All the little bumps and scrapes have been buffed out, and Eve had a new transmission put in just last year.

I'm a solid fifteen minutes out of town when I go to plug my phone into the aux cord. Shock and a mild amount of horror fill me when I realize I left it at the shop face down on the desk.

Poor Hazel.

And poor me. Nothing like a nine-hour road trip with only the radio and my thoughts to keep me company. Fuck's sake.

Could this month get any worse?

Good thing I know where the spa is.

Chapter 10

Eli

SHE'S IGNORING ME. I MEAN, I DON'T BLAME HER, BUT I need to see her. I've been trying to figure out a way to explain myself for weeks now. How do I tell her what happened? How do I convince her that I needed a little time? That I can make things work if she's willing to try again.

I wouldn't blame her if she didn't forgive me. Hell, I wouldn't blame her if she never spoke to me again. Right now, though, I need to know what's going through her mind.

It's the middle of the day on a Tuesday, which means she should be at the shop—the shop I've been avoiding like a coward. How does one come back from that? I kicked her out of my house after having sex, as I spun wild stories in my head about being a cheating husband while she ran out of there crying, with tears streaming down her face. It's unforgivable.

The worst part? Lara was the kind of person who'd want me to move on. She told me one night when we were tucked into bed together, that if she ever left before me, I was to find someone else. Someone young, hot, and funny.

Lara wanted me happy, more than anything else in the world, and I...I ran away at the first sign of it.

When Lara died, I lost the best thing that ever happened to me. What if it happens again? What if having Tucker is supposed to be enough? It feels greedy to have more.

"Well, I gave up calling and went by the house, but she's not there. And why does it look like she's been sleeping on the couch?" Hazel's voice rings through the shop the second I yank the door open. If there wasn't a goddamn bell attached to it, I would've snuck right back outside. Hazel is...a lot.

"Oh no you don't, asshole. Get your fine ass in here and start explaining what the fuck is going on." Hazel pins me with a glare. Chuck Massy's eyes widen, a hand barely hiding the smile he's trying so desperately to smother.

"What's wrong this time, Haze?"

"Don't you *Haze* me." Her eyes narrow, hands gripping her hips. "Our beloved Sibby has gone missing, and you two have been weird for weeks."

"She's right about that." Chuck cocks his head.

"What do you mean by missing?"

"She's ignoring my calls. When I called here, Chuck said she left for the day—nay, the next two days. So I stopped by her house, but she's not there. Her comforter and pillows are on the couch."

My heart cracks in half, knowing I'm the cause of Sibyl's pain—the reason she's avoiding her bedroom, avoiding me, and by extension, Tucker. My boy misses her something fierce. And it's all my fault.

"Dad!" Kellan's voice booms when he runs in from the shop. "Where's Sibyl's car?"

Chuck shrugs. "She said you put it out."

"Fuck." Kellan runs a hand through his hair. "I didn't finish! I just needed the space."

"Shit." Chuck reaches for the landline, dialing her number.

We wait, holding our breaths. Then the sound of a phone vibrating on the desk, makes my heart drop into my stomach.

"So that's what was buzzing," Chuck mumbles.

"Fuck!" Kellan turns to look at Hazel the moment her gasp echoes through the room. "What the fuck are you two doing here?"

Hazel is stuck staring at her phone, unintelligible squeaks coming out of her mouth.

"I'm just looking for Sybil." I shrug.

"Why? You two haven't talked in weeks." Kellan glares at me, crossing his arms over his chest.

"I know why!" Hazel screeches, shoving her phone under Kellan's nose.

I have an idea what she's looking at. It's not until Kellan's face turns a shade of red so deep it looks purple that I know for sure they're watching the video. I haven't seen it, but I saw a photo in the email we got. I've only seen the cover photo of the gallery Ramona sent us. We're in the water, and Sibyl is smiling at me like I hung the moon. My hand is cupping the side of her face, eyes trained on her.

I took a screenshot, not ready to see the rest of the gallery. But I got annoyed opening the email every time I wanted to see it—to see her looking at me like that.

I kissed her so much that afternoon. I wonder if the video is just five minutes straight of us making out.

"You son of a bi—" Kellan comes at me, his arm cranked back like he's going to hit me when Chuck clears his throat.

"What's Juniper Hills?" He's staring at the screen on

Sybil's bright pink cell phone, eyes creased with worry. "And why is she applying for a job there?"

"Shit." Hazel whips her head back to me. "What did you do, Logan?"

"Nothing worth mentioning to you," I grumble, heading for the door.

"Now wait a damn minute!" Kellan stomps after me, with Hazel on his heels, and Chuck flipping the closed sign on the shop. "Where are you going?" Kellan grabs my arm, spinning me around. I half expect his fist to crack my jaw open.

"I'm going after Sib." I wave an arm at my truck.

"Well, let's go then." Chuck gets in my front seat, Hazel and Kellan climbing in the back.

Goddamn this weird ass family.

"Sooo..." Hazel leans forward on the center console. "What'd you do? Huh?"

"I fucked up," I grumble.

Backing onto the main road, I drive toward the highway.

"I'll say." Kellan glares at me in the rearview mirror.

"Kissing her wasn't the mistake."

"That's debatable," he grunts.

"I didn't know she'd be the match at that photoshoot. I had no idea she even liked me. The second I turned around, though, something just...clicked."

"You didn't know she likes you?" Kellan looks incredulous.

"I had no—"

"What's Juniper Hills?" Chuck interrupts.

"It's a fancy spa," I say.

"Rich-people spa," Hazel says at the same time. "How do you know about it?" she gasps, her head whipping my direction.

"Lara loved it," I whisper.

"Oh." Hazel pats my shoulder, swiping over to answer as her phone rings. "Hello, lover."

"Don't hello lover me!" Taylor's voice crackles over the speakerphone. "Why is your GPS moving out of town, and why did I see you in Logan's truck, with not one but three guys that aren't me?"

"It's not three random guys." Hazel rolls her eyes, a wicked smile on her face.

"Hey, T, can you get Tuck from school today?" I glance down at the phone, surprised to see Taylor's face glaring at me.

"Can I pick up your son while you abscond with my wife? No. Call Tori. I'm coming after you guys."

"No, you are not," Hazel growls. "We're going after Sibby. No need to get all possessive. It's literally Dad Massy, and these two goons, who you know I loathe more than I like."

"Baby, we've talked about this. You can't just run around with other guys. I can't—"

"I'll make it up to you tonight." Hazel drops her voice low and suggestive.

"Fine. I'll grab Tucker. What time will you be back?"

"Depends on how far she made it." Kellan pipes up from the backseat.

"Alright, fine. Take care of my wife, assholes."

Chuck clears his throat.

"Not you, Dad." Taylor hangs up the phone real quick.

We've all called Chuck, dad, since high school. The Massy house was the place we hung out. When our shitty home lives became too much, he was the dad we needed. The safe space. It's where Taylor met Hazel.

Shit, my first date with Lara was to a family dinner at

the Massy house. I was fascinated by their dynamic, seeing people who actually loved each other. Lara's family was like that, too. She thought I was adorable, bringing her to their family dinner. She took me to hers the next week, and that was the night I fell in love with her.

Her rosy cheeks and freckles flash into my mind. Her bright smile, curly hair. Just like always, that happy smiling face I fell in love with turns gray. Lifeless. Those curls I loved so much spread out around her like a halo, covering the table.

A moan rips from my chest; a sob stuck in my throat as I park the truck on the side of the road. Kellan follows me out. He's seen me like this before. Talked me through a panic attack once or twice. Let me cry without issuing a single judgment.

My hands find my knees, breath coming in shaky as I try to push the image aside. The last time I saw her, laid out on a fucking table where I had to tell the police, "Yes, that is Lara Logan. Mother of my child, love of my life. Dead on a table."

"I can't—" I grab Kellan's arms, pleading with my eyes. "I can't do it again."

"I know, Bud." Kellan hauls me into his chest. He's a big dude, built like his dad, which is to say, like a bear. Kellan and Chuck have to be at least two fifty a piece, coming in somewhere around six foot three or four. I've never asked, knowing the answer would make my six-two feel short.

He waits until my breathing is back to normal, then clasps me on both shoulders.

"You know I can't tell you that everything will be alright. I can't tell you nothing is going to happen to her, but I can tell you that you'd never find someone better than my sister. If you're serious about settling down with someone again, she's worth the risk."

"I know." I'm barely able to whisper. I know I'll never find better, because she is the best. She's the one for us, and we've fucking missed her. I know what it feels like to lose someone, to have to come to terms with never seeing them again, and I refuse to do that with her. As long as we're both breathing, I will do everything in my power to keep her.

"Then let's go find her." Kellan grins, shoving me toward the back door of the pickup. He climbs behind the wheel, and we continue down the road.

Chapter 11

Eli

"You love her, don't you?" Hazel turns her back to the window, her gaze stripping me bare.

"I don't understand it." I look down at my hands.

"Son, you've loved Sybil her whole life." Chuck turns to the back of the truck, his voice gentle.

"No." I shake my head, feeling small. "I love Lara."

"Of course you do." Hazel grips my hand.

"I'm not saying it's always been the same kind of love." Chuck reaches behind the driver's seat and pats my knee. "I'm thinking you just picked up on the *in love* part, but you've always loved her. Some part of you. And you'll always love Lara."

I snap my gaze to him. Chuck would know. He lost his wife when Sybil was born. She died in childbirth. "You don't have to stop loving Lara to allow Sybil into your heart. You and that boy have got enough love to go around for the both of them. Trust me."

"I feel like I'm cheating on her—on her memory." The weight of it curves my shoulders forward.

Kellan groans from the driver's seat. "Ugh, are you boning my sister?"

Hazel squeals from beside me. "He totally is! You saw the video."

I roll my eyes. My gaze drifts to the blurring trees out the window.

"Lara loved you, Eli. More than anything, she wanted you to be happy. So be happy." Chuck pats my knee again, settling back into his seat.

"You should text Karen." Hazel winks when I side-eye her. "She'll tell you the same thing, but I bet you'd feel better hearing it from her."

I tap my finger on the door of the truck, nodding to myself before I pull out my cell phone and text my mother-in-law.

ME

Hey Karen

Sorry to bother you, but I need to ask you a question

KAREN

Eli! How are you sweetheart? Dad and I were just talking about our trip coming up. We can't wait to see you and Tucker.

ME

Tucker talks about it constantly. He can't wait to see you both.

We're doing well. Thanks

KAREN

Good. We're going to spoil the heck out of him while we're there.

ME

😅 I'm sure you will

I set my phone back down, unable to formulate the words I need to ask her. Karen and Joe are the only people I talk to about Lara. It's too hard to avoid it altogether with them, but I can't bring myself to mention her around others either. People don't really want to hear about my dead wife, right?

KAREN

What's up honey? You said you had a question

ME

I don't know how to ask. It's not even really a question

KAREN

Color me intrigued kiddo. What's on your mind?

ME

I think I met someone…

KAREN

Oh!! I am so thrilled for you!! Who is it? Do we know her?

ME

It's Sibyl

KAREN

SIBYL MASSY?

Honey… Sibyl is perfect for you and Tucker.

I chuckle. Did everyone know it but me? It certainly feels that way, now that I see her.

KAREN

What's the question though?

ME

It feels wrong?

KAREN

Because she's Kellan's sister?

ME

No. Because I have a wife.

KAREN

Oh.

Listen I can only imagine how hard this might be for you. But Lara would want you to be happy.

ME

Isn't it too soon

to feel like this?

KAREN

You've known her for your whole life. I don't think your feelings are new.

But hon. If you wait until you feel ready you're never going to move forward. Not with Sibyl and not with anyone else.

Personally I hope it's with Sibyl. I adore her. And she adores both of you. What more could this grandma ask for?

ME

How is no one but me shocked by how fast this happened?

KAREN

Eli. You and Lara got married three months after you met on Tinder... realizing you're in love with a girl who you've been friends with for over twenty years isn't a surprise.

ME

I'm kind of kicking myself that it took so long to see it

KAREN

 I bet you are, kid.

Give yourself some grace. On both accounts.

ME

I'll try. Thanks Mom

KAREN

Anytime hon. You know we're always here for you.

Hopefully we'll be seeing more of Sibyl on this next trip then??

ME

It really doesn't bother you?

KAREN

No Eli. It really doesn't bother us.

We want you and Tucker to be happy. If that just happens to be with the incredible Sibyl Massy who are we to question it?

ME

She'll be around then. If I can find her to apologize

KAREN

grovel if you have to. Sibyl is a special one

ME

That she is

Hazel's squeal pulls me away from my phone. The earsplitting sound makes all of us flinch.

"You guys have over a million views and counting!" She shoves her phone under my nose. Sibyl and I appear on the screen. The video is less than a minute-long, but I feel every single heated stare. Every stolen kiss, every earth-shattering smile, like it's still happening.

I told Sibyl I needed to make her mine, and it's never felt truer than in this moment. I was stupid to let her go, stupid to wish I'd never let it go that far. Truth is, it'll never be enough where Sibyl is concerned.

I need her in my life. In my house. On my bed. In my arms. Mine. I don't think I've ever needed anything more. Ever.

SEXY HUNKY MAN 💀💀
SEXY HUNKY MAN 💀💀 SENT A LINK

Looks like your plan worked, huh?

"Your plan?" I pass Hazel her phone back, one eyebrow raised in her direction.

"Oh shit." Her eyes widen as she locks the screen, and tucks her phone away.

"You did this?"

"I...might have?" she grins. "I mean, I didn't know for sure you'd get matched with Sibby, but I *hoped* you would."

"Nobody thought to ask me about this?" Kellan grumbles.

"Sibyl doesn't need your *permission.*" Hazel reaches forward to whack him on the shoulder.

"Jesus." I blow out a breath and run my hand through my hair, chuckling. "Guess I owe you a thank-you then."

Hazel squeals, throwing her arms around me in an awkward hug. "I'm so excited for you two. You're the best people I know! You deserve to be happy together."

I give her a smile, my eyes locking with Kellan's in the rearview.

"Don't think I won't knock you out if you break her heart," he grumbles.

"I wouldn't expect anything less. I seem to recall bruising a few faces with you over the years."

"Yeah, well, I was hoping you'd continue being oblivious to how hard she's been crushing on you."

"Jesus, did everyone know but me?"

"Apparently." Chuck cackles from the front seat. "We shoulda made a bet about these two." He peers back to wink at me.

"Well, Taylor knows. So, the whole town is about to know." Hazel grins, her face still tipped down at her phone.

"Maybe we should refocus on trying to get her back."

"I'd still like to know what you did that sent her running." Kellan's eyes narrow at me in the mirror.

"Trust me," I groan. "You don't."

"Shit," Hazel sighs. "Now I have to know."

"You'll have to try to wring it from her then. I'm taking this shit to the grave."

Chapter 12

Sibyl

The door to the Alemoor Diner jingles. It's been jingling nonstop for the past fifteen minutes. Apparently, this is a busy place.

Alemoor is the place to come for pie. Tourists actually come here for their pie. It's good, I guess. I have three different flavors in front of me, and none of them is really shocking me with their fruity fillings and subpar crusts.

I made it the whole twenty miles to Alemoor before realizing my car was, in fact, not fixed. Kellan would kill me if I drove the full nine hours in it. That is, if the car didn't off me on the way.

I shovel a massive bite of peach pie into my gob at the same time a very deep, very familiar voice says, "This seat taken?"

My jaw drops, the pie evacuating like it's sentient and knows it's either the plate or stomach acid.

"What're you doing here?" My voice squeaks out, eyes growing wide as I watch Eli fold himself into the booth beside me.

"Where you headed?" He looks at the assortment of

half-eaten pie slices, then tugs the piece of apple toward him.

"Nowhere, I'm just eating pie." I shrug, twirling my fork in the carnage of the peach pie.

"Not running away?"

I gasp. "First of all, rude. Second—"

"I stressed you out enough that you need a spa day?"

I glance at him, hating that a smile so easily splits my lips. Damn him. Eli slides my phone over the table, while a serious look takes over his face.

"I'm so sorry." His hand reaches for mine.

I don't pull away because I'm desperate to feel him. To be wanted by him.

"I'm so fucking sorry. Please don't leave. Don't move because I'm an asshole."

I shake my head, tears spilling down my cheeks. "I shouldn't have—"

"No, Baby." He scoots closer, pulling me into him as best he can in the tiny diner booth. "I panicked. I've never..." He blows out a breath, the force of it moving my hair. "I've never brought anyone home before. Never had anyone in our room before."

"I know." I tilt my head, needing to see his eyes. "It's okay. I will never replace her. I'd never try to. And I can't compete with her either, the love you guys had..." I shift my gaze back to the pie. "She is your perfect someone, and I can respect that. I—I get it. It's okay if you can't—"

"We want *you*," Eli whispers, gently shifting me to face him. "Lara *was* my perfect person. I needed her at nineteen. But you..." He shakes his head, incredulous. "You're perfect for who I am now."

"I am?"

"Yeah, you are." Eli tilts my head, bringing his lips down

to meet mine. It's slow and exploratory—the ease of three weeks ago slips back in.

Hope blooms deep in my chest, freezing solid when I replay the way he looked at me with such panic and horror.

"Wait," I whisper, hands on his chest, pushing him back.

He releases my hair and lets me move back far enough that he can see my face, but doesn't let me go completely, as if he can't bring himself to stop touching me, afraid I might disappear.

"We should slow down, get to kno—"

"I know you. I don't need to slow down. You are what I want."

"You said that. Everyone says that, but it's never me they pick in the end. You can't even bring me home. You need time. You need—"

"You," he interrupts again. A smile turns the corners of his lips up. "I have more I need to work through, I know that. But I just want you. I needed—I just needed to know it was okay to want you. I know that sounds stupid, I know I'm an adult, and I can do what I want. But I talked to your dad, and I texted Lara's mom. They both told me the same thing."

"What's that?"

"That Lara wanted me to be happy, always. And you make me happy."

"I don't want to make your life harder. I don't want to hurt you."

"You're not, I swear." He trails his fingers down my face, a soft, dopey smile on his.

"Eli..."

He holds a finger up, fishing out his phone before

dialing a number. Victoria's voice chirping through the speaker.

"Tori, it's Eli."

"Obviously." Hazel's twin *sounds* like she's rolling her eyes. "What do you want, Logan? I'm pretty sure we're supposed to be mad at you or something."

Eli rolls his eyes at me, a grin splitting his lips wide. "What do you have on the market that Sibby might like?"

"What?" Tori shrieks on the other line. I stare at him, wide-eyed. He's talking about buying a house—for *me*? For us. This man is certifiable.

I panic, jamming my finger onto the *end-call* button. "Elijah Henry Logan, what are you doing?"

"Buying us a house," he says, as if it's obvious.

"You can't buy us a house!"

"Will you come stay with me then? Move in, be with me."

"Move in?" I throw my hands up, eyes wide. "Are you insane?"

"For you? Definitely."

"How's it going?" Hazel appears at the edge of the table, her voice sing-song.

"What? How are you here?" I gape, my eyes scanning the diner to find not only my dad, but also my brother as well, both of them demolishing a piece of pie.

"Why is my sister calling you?" Hazel looks at Eli's phone on the table.

"He's trying to buy me a house!" I shake my head.

"Ooh, did you tell him you already have one?"

"She doesn't have a house." Eli rolls his eyes. "She has a hovel."

"Hey! It's small, but it's not a hovel." I burn with indignation.

Hazel snorts, dropping onto the bench opposite us. "She lives in the carriage house. Sibby's been trying to renovate the big house by herself for years now."

I feel my cheeks heat. Eli's eyes widen when they meet mine. I can see him trying to work it out. Trying to figure out which house Hazel's talking about.

My street was, and still kind of is, filled with retired folks. Most of them are selling their houses to move into retirement communities. There are currently four vacant houses, and three on the market. The carriage house is tucked between two massive old Victorian homes, but it has its own lot. It's why I bought the house. I love the main one, but I also fell in love with the tiny house next door.

I know for a fact Eli's been too busy to pay attention to the real estate on my side of town. His construction business has been busy the past several years building a new development on the east side—cookie-cutter houses that hold zero charm compared to the older neighborhood I live in.

Not that I don't think Eli's crew builds great houses. I'm sure they're fine.

I groan, my thought spiral ending abruptly when his head tilts to the side. My body is ready to crumble under the weight of his gaze. His eyes have narrowed, bright green irises judging me.

"Please tell me it's not the purple one. Aside from the color, that place is a fucking disaster." Eli sighs.

"Give her *some* credit." Hazel rolls her eyes.

He smiles. "How much have you renovated?"

"Uh...the guest bath?" I cringe.

Renovations are hard. They tell you to measure twice, cut once, but I've had to take multiple trips to the hardware store for the same three pieces—more than one time. I'm not great with power tools, but my pride would absolutely not allow me to concede to Taylor and Kellan's assertion that I'd be needing their help.

"I wanna see it." Eli jumps out of the booth, offering me his hand.

"What? Now?" I stare at him. This is wildly out of hand at this point.

"Yeah, now. I get the feeling the faster we fix that place up, the faster I'll convince you to move in with us."

"*Move in?*" Hazel screeches. The entire restaurant stares at us.

"She won't move in with me." Eli pouts.

"We had one night together. You don't move in with someone after one night!"

I look to Hazel, instantly regretting it. The little shit is going to take his side on this one.

"I mean...it's not like he's an actual stranger..."

"Jesus Christ." I rub my temples. "You people are impossible."

"I tried to tell her I don't need to get to know her." Eli leans on the back of the booth, winking.

"You also kicked me out of the house after we had sex..." I volley back, regretting it the second he cringes.

"Oh my God, Logan. What the fuck?" Hazel's fists curl on the table top.

"I panicked." He shoots her a menacing glare, then squats beside the booth, taking my hand in both of his. His eyes don't leave mine, and the sincerity in that gaze takes my breath away. "You surprised the hell out of me. I wasn't expecting it to hit so hard, or so fast. But your dad's right—part of me has always loved you. I don't know when that turned into being in love with you, probably the moment I spun around and saw you in that dress at the photo shoot. But I do love you. I am in love with you."

Chapter 13

Eli

"I CAN LOVE YOU BOTH," I WHISPER, MY VOICE GROWING desperate.

I just told Sibyl I'm in love with her, and she's...staring at me. Her eyes unblinking, growing silvery with tears.

"I can't replace her," she finally whispers. Her voice barely audible over the sounds of the diner.

"I'm not asking you to. I don't want you to be Lara. I want you, Sibyl Massy, just the way you are."

"I'm scared you'll change your mind. What if, in six months, you wake up and realize this is not what you wanted?"

"Not gonna happen. I swear to you, it's not going to happen."

"But it could! You could hate the way I sleep, or get annoyed at the way I breathe. Or...I don't know. What if I clip my toenails on the bathroom floor and they stab the bottoms of your feet and you're constantly having to yell at me for it?"

"*Do* you leave toenail clippings on the floor?" Hazel leans forward, her eyes wide.

"Of course not," Sibyl hisses at her.

"Hazel." I turn to pin her with a glare. "You wanna fuck off now?"

Hazel scoffs. "I certainly do not."

"Haze, the cherry pie is good." Sibyl smiles at her.

"Sibs, I love you, but I do not want pie right now." Hazel crinkles her nose at us.

"Hazel," I bark. "Go away."

"Sheesh, fine. I'm going. Don't have to get all grumpy about it." Hazel rolls her eyes at me, slips out of the booth, joins the other tagalongs at the bar, and steals Kellan's pie.

"Sibyl, relationships are about compromise. It's not going to be perfect—none of them are. But that doesn't mean it's not worth it."

"You and Lara were perfect, though. Your expectations have to be sky-high."

A laugh bursts out of me. "We were not perfect—at all. We fought all the time. Lara was constantly mad at me for something. We didn't love each other any less because of it. We chose to work through those problems together."

"This feels crazy. Doesn't it feel crazy to you?"

"Yeah, it does. Crazy in a good way. Crazy like I'm the luckiest guy in the world that you'd even want to spend time with me."

"Of course I want to spend time with you. You're one of my best friends, and I love that little boy."

My chest warms, heart expanding like a hot air balloon. "He loves you, too. We both do."

Her cheeks flush, a blush works up her neck—all the way to the tips of her ears.

"I've loved you for as long as I can remember," she whispers, her eyes glancing through long lashes.

"And I'm sorry it took me so long to figure that out." I

slide my hand up her jaw, fingers cupping the back of her neck. "I don't need time to know that I want you in my life. If I didn't think it'd send you running for the hills, I'd take you to Prescott's and get you a ring right now. It'll never be enough—the time I get with you. I know the way loss can sneak up on us. I know we're not guaranteed tomorrow, and I'm not about to waste any more precious seconds when you could be mine."

She works through a swallow, her head bobbing on a nod. "Then date me, you crazy person. Don't jump straight to marriage and living together. Date me, until the house is ready. And then, if you haven't changed your mind and you're sure you want to leave the house with all of Lara's memories, we'll move into the big house."

"Deal." I smile into her mouth, pressing my lips into hers. Sibyl greets me, her body surging into mine. The kiss devolves into something more needy, hungrier than it started.

Hazel's voice goes up in a cheer, drowning out the sound of someone hacking. I'd bet anything it's Kellan, choking on a bite of pie.

"Should we make a run for it?" I whisper.

"My keys are in the cupholder..." She grins, mischievous eyes meeting mine. "It should probably be towed, though." She grimaces. "Turns out Kellan didn't fix it after all."

"What's wrong with it, exactly?" I ask, offering her a hand as I haul myself out of the booth.

"The brakes don't work one hundred percent of the time..." She gives me a nervous smile.

"Jesus." I wrap an arm around her shoulders, hauling her into my side. "I'm going to have words with your brother. You can't drive something that isn't safe."

"He's hoping that if he takes long enough, I'll give up and buy something new."

"Didn't he just put a transmission in?"

"I did." Kellan pops up behind us. "I'm tired of fixing the same car. I'm a body guy, Sibs. I hate mechanic work."

"Ahh," Sibyl croons, looking back at Kellan as we make our way out the door. "But you're so good at it."

Kellan narrows his eyes at her.

"Hey, Dad." Sibyl smiles at Chuck. I let her go so she can hug him. "Sorry to scare you guys."

"That's okay, Sugar Plum." Chuck gives her a toothy grin before jumping into the passenger seat again.

Sibyl glances at her car, a little pout on her face.

"I'll have it towed." I run my thumb along her pouty lip.

"Okay," she concedes, following Hazel into the backseat.

"Did you watch the video?" Hazel practically shouts at Sibyl.

"Hey, man." Kellan stops me at the driver's side door. "You sure about this? About her?"

"I am." I nod.

"Hell yeah." He pulls me into a hug. "It's about time!"

"Weren't you just about to punch me at the shop?"

"That was just my initial reaction to seeing you kiss my sister. Let's try to do that as little as possible. Yeah?"

"Cover your eyes then." I wink, climbing into the truck next to Sibyl. "I don't plan on wasting a single second not kissing your sister."

Kellan groans, uttering curses as he pulls himself into the driver's seat. "This is going to be a problem, isn't it?"

Sibyl gives him a shit-eating grin. "More like my new life mission."

Cool, soft fingers weave through my hair, pulling me

into her. Pillowy lips tug at mine with a tenderness I'm still not used to. Chuck whistles, Hazel whoops beside us.

"Alright, we get it. You're a thing now," Kellan groans. "Stop it, Sibs, please."

Sibyl giggles, trying to pull back, but I swing her onto my lap, flashbacks of that afternoon play in my mind—the way she rode my hand, right there in the parking lot. God, this girl was made for me.

"Hey," she whispers, dark hair dropping like a curtain between us and the rest of the truck.

"Hey, gorgeous, I've been missing you."

"I've been missing you, too. I miss Tucker." Her sweet voice breaks, sending a dagger straight through my heart.

"Baby." I swipe a tear off her cheek. "I'm so sorry. He's missing you, too."

"Can I come home with you tonight? I want to see him."

A weight lifts off my chest as I tuck her into me. "You can come over whenever you want. Stay as long as you want."

She chuckles, burying her face into my neck, as one hand reaches up to trace a path down my face.

"I like the beard," she muses, fingers scratching my facial hair.

I haven't had a beard since Lara died. She always liked me with facial hair. The past three weeks, I haven't had it in me for a full shave. I've trimmed it once or twice, but this is the longest I've ever let it go. All my downtime has consisted of trying to figure out how to get here: with Sibyl in my lap, and some kind of plan for the future.

The one where I get to keep her.

Chapter 14

Sibyl

"Sibby!" Tucker crashes into my legs, his little arms wrapping around me. I scoop him up, burying my face in his neck. God, I missed him so much. I missed Eli, too, I did, but this kid is the highlight of my day.

There have been very few days in the last four years that I haven't seen him. This is the longest I've spent away from him, and it about killed me. I knew I had a crush on Eli, but I think I've been in love with this little boy since the day I met him. I remember thinking how perfect Lara and Eli had done.

I don't know when I started to see him as mine, but now that it's an option? There's no denying how I feel about them both. I want to be theirs, and I want them to be mine.

"Hey Buddy, I missed you." I smack a kiss on his cheek, smoothing his wild curls off his face. He has hair like his mama. Unruly and beautiful, just like she was.

"I thought you were mad at me." Tucker pulls away, looking down at his feet. His hands tangle around each other, and nervous energy buzzes around him.

"No way. Why would you think that?"

"I made you stay to read that story. I woke up, and I saw you leave. You were crying, you—"

"That was my fault." Eli kneels beside us, putting a hand on Tucker's shoulder. "I made her cry."

"But why?"

"Because I was scared."

Air whooshes out of me at Eli's confession. I guess we're doing this now.

"You're not scared of anything," Tucker scoffs.

"I am, though." Eli ruffles his hair, leaning against the couch. "I know you don't remember her, Buddy, but I loved your mom."

Tucker folds himself onto the floor, tugging me down with him. He leans into me, one little hand clutching mine, his face somber. Even he knows how rare it is for Eli to talk about Lara.

"When I lost her..." Eli sits forward, picking at the seam of his jeans. "It was really hard for me. I had a rough couple of years."

"Because you missed her?"

"Yeah." Eli sighs.

"I'm sorry you're sad, Dad."

"Thanks, Buddy. It's not your fault. I am so happy to be your dad."

"I know." Tucker reaches out to pat Eli's hand. "I'm still sorry you're sad."

I squeeze Tucker's hand, giving Eli what I hope is an encouraging look.

"The reason I was scared—the reason I made Sibyl cry—is because I realized that I love her."

Tucker's jaw hits the ground, his eyes bounce between us.

"I got scared that I would lose her, too. Scared I might make your mom sad, if I love someone new."

"Sibyl's not new." Tucker's head cocks to the side, contemplating.

"No, she's not. But the way I feel for her is new."

"You love her?"

"I do." Eli peers over Tucker's head, green eyes piercing into mine.

"Sibby, do you love my dad?"

"I do." I glance at Tucker.

A wide, toothy grin spreads across his face, then worry clouds his little eyes as his hand pulls from mine. "Will my mom be sad if I love you, Sibyl?"

"No," Eli and I whisper at the same time.

"I don't want to make her sad. You said she's always with us." Tucker's baby blues turn to Eli.

"She is. She watches over you, and she just wants you to be happy. She'd never be sad if you loved Sibyl. She loved Sibyl too, in her own way."

Tears fill my eyes at the memories of all of us together. Lara fit right in. From the moment we met her, we all loved her. Every single one of us. I'd come to terms with my unrequited crush years before she came around. I was happy for them—happy that Eli had found someone so perfect for him.

I glance at him. There's a soft smile on his face. One big hand comes up to wipe the tears off my cheeks.

"So we can all love Sibby?" Tucker asks, voice hopeful.

"We can, and we do. Don't we, Bud?"

"Yeah, but I love her more. She was my girl first."

A laugh bursts from Eli, light and sweet. The kind of laugh he used to give so freely. It wraps around me like a warm summer day.

"Maybe she can be both of ours." Eli ruffles Tucker's hair before his hand reaches for mine.

"Sibyl, do you wanna be our girl?" Tucker's sweet face turns toward me.

"If you'll have me." I grin.

"We'll have you." Eli's voice softens. He leans forward, pressing a tender kiss to my lips.

"Wait, Dad. What about the girl you went on a date with?" Tucker's eyes widen, as if he just remembered.

"Funny story, kiddo." Eli grins. "Sybil was the girl."

"What?!" Tucker squeals. "You didn't tell me that!"

"Yeah, because you can't keep a secret." Eli hauls his little boy into his lap, tickling him until we dissolve into giggles.

We spend all night snuggled in together. Tucker makes us take turns telling funny stories. Eli has all the good ones about Taylor and Kellan, while I have a few of my own about him, both of us recalling fun memories of Tucker.

We talk so long that Tucker falls asleep cradled between us on Eli's bed, with one chubby little hand wrapped around mine.

"Hey," Eli rasps. His fingers tuck a hair behind my ear as he jerks his head toward the door.

I shimmy out from underneath Tucker, following Eli back down to the main level. He pulls me onto his lap, settling into the couch with me in his arms.

"You know I'm never letting you go now, right?" His breath tickles my skin. Goosebumps cascade down my arms.

"I sure hope not," I whisper.

Eli's hand trails down my spine, sending another shiver through me.

"I want to taste you," he murmurs into my neck, his tongue flattening as it drags up my throat. I think I might whimper. "Can I taste you?"

Eli slides one hand into my hair, his fingers tightening into a fist. Tugging gently, he bares my neck, lips sealing around my pulse point. His other hand slides between my legs, pressing into the seam of my leggings.

"Yes," I breathe. At this point, I think I'd say yes to anything he asked me.

I am so far gone for this man.

Eli lies me on my back, slowly stripping my clothes off, fingers trailing across my skin. I gasp as they ghost over my ribs. The sensation is almost too much to bear.

"Fuck me. You're so fucking pretty." Warm calloused palms slip beneath me, his fingers unclasping my bra. One hand spreads out across my rib cage, the other braces the couch as he leans down, taking my nipple between his teeth.

My back arcs into the cushions, chest pressing into him. His tongue laves, lips locking around my nipple, sucking until it's a hardened peak.

He trails kisses across my chest, moving to my other breast.

I moan, sinking my hands into his hair, tugging to pull his face to mine. Our lips meet in a messy kiss. Teeth clacking, bodies surging to meet each other.

"No," I whine, trying to hold Eli's face to mine when he pulls away.

"I'll make it worth your while. I promise."

"Fine," I grumble, relenting.

I watch him slip down my body, one knee dropping to

the ground as he plants himself between my legs, spreading me open.

He groans. "You're fucking soaked."

"Mmm," I hum. "Have been from the moment I heard your voice at the diner."

"Fuck me," he whispers, swiping one finger through my slick heat. "So fucking pretty," he mutters, moving closer until his mouth is on me.

His tongue tastes every inch of my pussy. I'm writhing by the time he comes up to my clit. Green eyes peer through his lashes, watching me as I start to spiral tighter and tighter.

He flicks my clit with the tip of his tongue, sending me over the edge. I chant his name, fingers gripping his hair. My hips thrust into his face, thighs shaking as he wrings every last drop of pleasure from me.

Chapter 15

Eli

"I DON'T KNOW HOW—" I WIPE MY MOUTH ACROSS Sibyl's upper thigh. Her arousal glinting in the low light. "I ever went without tasting you."

Her cheeks flush, chest heaving from the aftermath of her orgasm.

"You're the sweetest thing I've ever tasted." I crawl up her body, waiting for the guilt, for the taste of betrayal—it never comes. The only taste in my mouth is Sibyl.

"I need you," she whispers. Her fingers work at the button on my jeans. I yank my shirt over my head with one hand, standing to kick out of my Levis.

Her eyes widen, growing darker when she realizes I've been walking around with no boxers on. When I got the text this morning from Ramona, I knew I couldn't wait any longer. I needed to fix things with her.

Now I'm standing before her, fisting my cock, drinking her in while she stares at me with hungry eyes.

Sitting on the couch, Sibyl licks her lips. She leans forward, hands gripping my thighs.

"Sibby, you do—"

My brain short-circuits. Sibyl's tongue flattens, sliding up the seam of my cock from root to tip. A little moan vibrates in her throat as she takes me in her mouth.

"Fuck," I groan, pitching forward. I catch myself on the couch, leather creaking under my hands as my grip tightens. My hips snap forward on instinct. Sibyl groans, tears slipping from the corners of her eyes as she takes me to the back of her throat. Her hand moves between my legs, cupping my balls.

"You keep doing that, and I'm going to come in your mouth." I slip my free hand into her hair, letting the soft strands sift through my fingers.

She takes me deeper, pulling away enough to swirl my tip with her tongue.

"Come here." I pull her off of me, then tuck her beneath me, my cock pressing at her entrance. "Fuck." I drop my head into her shoulder. "Condoms are in my room."

"Don't need one." Sibyl tilts her hips, sucking my cock in deeper. "I've had you without one. There's no going back now."

"Fuck me," I groan, seating myself in her fully.

Yeah, fuck the condoms. This is...fuck, it's too much. I can feel everything—all her heat, her ridges. Every little piece of her. I rock into her, setting a slow pace, taking my time to memorize every inch of her.

"Oh God." She wraps her legs around my waist, changing the angle, pulling me even deeper.

Tingles dance at the base of my spine, my balls draw tight. I'll be damned if I'm going to come before she gets to again. Tilting my hips forward, I grind my pubic bone into her. Her gasp nearly undoes me as her muscles clench around me.

"Eli, Eli, Eli." She chants my name with a dreamy look on her face.

I'm panting as my release spills out of me, filling her up.

"Fuck, Baby." I collapse into her, burying my face in her neck, breathing her in. I take a moment to come down with her in my arms. This is how it should have been three weeks ago—slow and sacred. Not ending in tears.

Leaning onto my elbows, I press a tender kiss to her pulse point. "Let me get you cleaned up."

I push up from the couch, pulling out of her, unable to rip my gaze away as I watch my cum leak down her inner thighs. My cock twitches, trying to thicken again. My hand reaches forward on its own accord, fingers pressing the fluid back inside of her, making sure she doesn't lose a single drop.

"When you're ready..." I lift my gaze to hers. Her eyes mirror the fire I feel burning through my veins. "I'm going to put my baby in you, and we're going to grow our family."

Sibyl moans, back arching into my touch. "Eli," she breathes. "Do you have a breeding kink?"

"Not until right this second," I whisper, tipping forward to press my lips with hers. "I don't think it's going anywhere until I get you pregnant."

"Fuck, why is that so hot?" she whimpers. Her fingers come up to pinch her nipples, thighs slamming shut around my hand, hips seeking friction.

"You need another one?"

"Yes," she whispers, her face turning away, as if she's embarrassed.

"Baby." I guide her gaze back to mine, tucking a string of hair behind her ear before I thrust my fingers inside of her. "You can have as many orgasms as you want. I love watching you come."

"Oh God," she cries out. Her body takes over as she rides my hand, seeking her next high.

"Take what you need. I got you."

I scissor my fingers inside of her, rubbing my thumb in circles on her clit, watching as she falls apart for me again.

"Stay right here." I peck a kiss on her temple, then slip my pants back on.

I head for the guest bath, my breath catching, like every time I step into this space. It is so overwhelmingly Lara—with the dark green wallpaper, deep red capped mushrooms, and forest vibes. Where Sibyl is all sunshine and sweetness, Lara was darker, complex, and moody.

I loved that about her. Loved every single thing about her. She was my home. My best friend. This house holds so many memories of her. So many spaces she touched. Places where I still see her. Sibyl's house won't take long to renovate, but I'm going to use that time to savor every single memory of Lara here—give her a proper goodbye.

My fingers toy with the deep burgundy hand towel on the wall, remembering Lara's face lighting up when she'd found the perfect shade.

"I miss you," I whisper. "We're going to be okay, though, Lara. I hope you know that."

I wet a washcloth with warm water, and carry it out to the living room.

"Did Tucker wake up?" Sibyl asks, wrapped in a throw blanket, all the way up to her chin.

"No." I smirk, slipping under the blanket to clean between her legs.

"I swore I heard you talking." Two little lines appear on her forehead. She's so fucking adorable.

"I was talking to Lara." I shrug.

"Oh." Her face softens. Those deep brown eyes glimmer with understanding.

"Told her Tuck and I are gonna be okay."

Sibyl nods. Sitting up, she cups my jaw, thumb stroking my cheek. "It's okay if you need more time, Eli. I understand."

I shake my head, tilting my face to kiss her palm. "I made you a deal, and I'll keep it. I'd move you in right now, if I thought you'd be okay with it."

"I know. I just think we should take some time, do the dating thing."

"You do realize I can drop all my other jobs to finish that house, right?"

Sibyl scoffs, smacking my arm. "You will not! I can't afford to pay you a living wage."

"Fine, but I'm enlisting the boys, and we'll have it done in no time."

"Ugh." Sibyl shudders. "Kellan and Taylor are going to make fun of me. They said I'd ask for their help."

"Is that why it's taken years, and you've only finished the bathroom? Because you didn't want to ask them for help?"

She grins at me, sheepish. "Yes?"

"You should've asked me. I would've helped. Probably would have even done it in secret."

"I didn't want to take you away from Tucker."

"I would've brought him with me. We could have done it all together."

"Well..." Sibyl lets the blanket fall, sitting to straddle me. "We still can."

"Dad?" Tucker's voice carries down the stairwell.

Sibyl squeaks, tumbling off my lap, wrapping the blanket around herself again.

"Comin', Bud." I pull Sibyl down the hall with me. "I'll get him settled in his room."

"Okay." Sibyl's mouth splits in a yawn.

"Come on." I scoop Tucker up into my arms.

"Is Sibby here?" He yawns into my shoulder.

"Yeah, she's still here."

"I like it when she's here."

He snuggles in deeper, one hand tucking between his body and my chest.

"Me too, Tuck. Me too."

Epilogue

Eli

THERE ARE MOMENTS IN OUR LIVES WE KNOW WE WILL never forget—moments that change us, shape us. Moments like the day I married Lara, or when the doctor put Tucker on her chest. Every single first milestone of his. The phone call when police asked me to come identify Lara's body. Turning around to see my best friend's sister at a stranger photo session.

Moments like this: waking up to the warmth of the sun shining on my face, my two perfect people asleep in the bed next to me, tucked safe and sound into the room customized just for us.

Tucker with his unruly curls, Sibyl with her swollen belly—our baby due to arrive in just a few weeks. I'm already thinking about when we'll have another. Seeing her pregnant, in the house we renovated together? It's unleashed a whole other fantasy life I didn't know I'd been craving.

She stretches like a cat, the rock on her finger reflecting the light from the window. We were planning to be married this fall, but with the baby coming, we pushed it back to next spring. Sibyl wanted to skip it altogether and get married at the courthouse. But marrying Lara is one of my favorite memories with her.

I want that with Sibyl.

I want her in the white dress, with Chuck walking her down the aisle. I want Tucker as the ring bearer, and Kellan holding our baby next to me. I even talked Karen into the mother-son dance with me. I skipped it last time, opting for a cheesy, choreographed dance with Taylor and Kellan.

My parents haven't been in my life since I moved out at sixteen. They weren't at my first wedding, and they won't be at this one, but it doesn't make a difference to me. Everyone I love will be there. Sibyl even has a photo of Lara picked out to put at the end of the aisle.

It's going to be everything.

Warm brown eyes peer over Tucker's head, the corners softening when they meet mine. "Hey," she whispers.

"Morning, Baby, how'd you sleep?"

"Good." She covers a yawn. "What time did we fall asleep?"

"*You* wracked out within the first three minutes of the movie. Tucker made it about halfway. I turned it off when I realized you both passed out."

"He's going to be pissed." Sibyl rubs a hand down her stomach, smirking when the little one inside kicks it. "This kid is an asshole."

"I'm gonna let you get away with that, for now, considering you're the one with a baby kicking the shit out of you. But there's no way that baby is an asshole, not with you as their mom."

"And this is why I'm ninety-eight percent certain this is a girl. She's already got you wrapped around her little fingers."

"Nah." I chuckle. "It's a boy, has to be. I won't survive being a girl dad."

"Iffa gurl," Tucker mutters, his face still turned into his pillow.

"Not you too!" I tickle him, relishing the giggles that start our mornings off.

Tucker has his own room down the hall, but Fridays have become movie nights. We make popcorn, pick out our favorite candies, and the three of us snuggle up in the primary bedroom for a family night. It's become my favorite part of the week. Mostly because waking up with these two on Saturday mornings feels like heaven.

"What's for breakfast?" Tucker asks, rolling into Sibyl, kissing her belly. "Good morning, baby. It's your brother."

Sibyl's eyes dart to mine, growing misty.

"Pancakes?" I ask, stretching my arms above my head.

"Ew. Not pancakes again."

"I thought you liked pancakes?" I stare at him.

"I'm a man now, Dad. I need meat."

Sibyl snorts, trying to hold back her laughter. Tucker's head bounces on her stomach as it shakes.

"Fine," I relent. "I'll make pancakes for Mom, and you can have bacon."

"Yes!" Tucker shoots up in the bed, fist pumping the air. "Bacon!" He launches off the mattress, tearing out of the room.

"My God," Sibyl groans, rolling herself to the edge of the mattress. "If I had half his energy, I'd be doing a hell of a lot better."

"Baby," I croon, walking around the bed to take her hands and help her up. "You're growing a baby from scratch, that takes a lot of work. And you're doing it so well."

Her cheeks flush, the same way they always pink when I praise her. God, I love this woman.

"I'm barely doing anything. I only have enough energy to eat and sleep most days."

"And you look gorgeous doing it."

"Stop trying to get in my pants. I'm a sure thing." She swats my chest, but doesn't push me away.

"Yeah, I'll never stop doing that." I brush my nose along her jaw, breathing her in. "You are stunning, my love. I mean that."

"Thank you." Her hands reach around my neck, pulling my face down to hers, parting my lips with a scorching kiss. She pulls away, leaving me panting, wanting more. "Now I want pancakes."

"Dad!" Tucker yells from the kitchen. "Mom, did you forget about the bacon?"

"We're coming, Bud." Sibyl shoots me a grin, hands absentmindedly rubbing her stomach.

"Sibby..." I drop my voice low, breathing into her ear. "I can't wait to get you alone tonight."

Heat flashes in her eyes. "Have any specific plans for me?"

"I do." I grin as we make our way to the stairs. "But you'll have to wait to find out."

She snorts, giving a pointed look at her stomach. "You realize you're terrible at waiting, right?"

A laugh bursts from me. "Fair point."

"Come on, guys!" Tucker rounds the banister, crashing into my legs.

"Bro!" I scoop him off his feet, dangling him by his knees. "Slow down, man. That could have been Mom."

"Sorry!" Tucker giggles.

I carry him like that, all the way to the kitchen. Pulling

out the ingredients for breakfast, I watch him and Sibyl set up for their morning craft.

She's started to crochet. We have tiny little booties and hats all over the house. Tucker has been really into painting lately. Sibyl got him a watercolor set for his birthday. Aside from family night and waking up next to them, watching them bond like this has to be in my top five favorite things.

I love everything about this life.

Pressing two fingers to my lips, I tap them to the photo of Lara on the fridge. "Love you," I whisper. "Alright." I clap my hands together. "Who's ready for breakfast?"

Acknowledgments

Firstly thank you to my fellow photographers who've blessed us with the viral stranger photo sessions! I love you all, but especially Brooke and Three Photography who shared the session that inspired this spicy little morsel.

Second, thank YOU the readers! A humble thank you to everyone who's taken the time to read this, thank you, from the bottom of my heart. Books would be nothing without people to read them, and I appreciate each and every one of you!

To my family, my husband and son, thank you for putting up with my crazy. With my last minute notes, and the times I've jolted out of bed to write a scene. You guys are my rock, and I don't know what I would do without you!

To my beta readers, thank you so much for fixing my plot holes and sticking with my ADHD ramblings. These stories are so much better because of you! Calli, I'm so sorry about the trauma the hole scene gave you!

To my editor, thank you, Zara, for being the best hype woman a girl could ask for! Seriously, I am so glad to have met you!

To Amanda, thank you for sticking with me through this author journey. I'm so glad I met you and get to call you friend! This journey hasn't been nearly as lonely, getting to walk it with you.

To my besties—the girl's night group—thank you for

supporting me and pushing me to chase this dream. I hope it's not too spicy for you! Also, maybe don't let the husbands read this one ;)

About the Author

Bailey Johnson is a contemporary romance author who loves all things coffee and baked goods. She lives in rural North Dakota with her husband, son, obese dog, three cats and an ever growing flock of chickens.

If she's not writing you can usually find her exploring the farm with her son, pursuing photography or out riding a borrowed horse. She's obsessed with all things cowboy and is really enjoying returning to her ranching roots. Even if it is only in fiction.

Also by Bailey Johnson

Pillow Talk: A Kane Ridge Ranch Novella

Don't Leave Me Behind

An Excerpt From Kane Ridge Ranch Book One

Don't Leave Me Behind

Clay

There's someone outside the cabin.

I swear I heard a car door thud. It was quiet, muffled, like someone parked far enough away that I'd be less likely to hear it. This feels like the beginning of a bad joke. I swear to God, if Adler is out there sneaking up on the cabin, I'm going to kill him. Slipping out of bed, I pad to the top of the stairs, squinting through the floor-to-ceiling windows at the front of Leni's cabin. The moon is high and bright, painting the landscape outside, but I still can't see anything that looks out of place.

Picking my way down the metal and wood staircase, I tiptoe over to the entry. It's possible that someone stopped along the highway and got out to take a piss, but I'm far enough from the road that I doubt I'd hear that. No, someone's on Kane land, real close to Leni's cabin. If they're here, expecting to find her asleep in her bed, they're in for a surprise.

A steady cadence of thuds indicates footsteps on the

deck. I scan the living room for a weapon, remembering at the last second that I cleaned my rifle when I got home from work tonight. Adrenaline floods my veins as I tiptoe into the kitchen, where my duty rifle leans against a white wooden chair. Moonlight glimmers off the freshly oiled barrel. The magazine sits on the kitchenette table next to it. Five rounds, that's as far as I got before I squirreled my attention away to dinner and left it for tomorrow. I grab the gun and feed the magazine into its slot, hoping whoever is outside doesn't hear the click as it snaps into place.

My fingers pull back the charging handle as a key slides into the lock. *Who the fuck has a key?* No one in the family would sneak in here, not in the middle of the night. They know it would be a bad idea.

So, who is messing with me tonight?

Keeping the rifle ready in my hands, I wait, trying to hear over the sound of my heart banging against my chest. Anticipation coils deep in my gut. There's a pause once the door opens, the moonlight illuminating a silhouette that doesn't look like any of the Kane boys or the ranch hands. I'm about to demand they identify themselves when there's a crash, and the intruder goes flying to the ground.

I shoulder the rifle, ready to defend myself, before flicking on the lights. It only takes a couple of blinks before I can clearly see what's in front of me, and I think my heart stops beating for a second, because here she is.

The girl I've been avoiding since I was twenty-one, only, this is not the eighteen-year-old girl I saw last...*holy shit*. She is breathtakingly beautiful. Air rips from my lungs as I take her in. Long brown hair fans out around her head, wispy bangs hanging on either side of her face. Those big green eyes looking up at me with confusion, her movements slow and apprehensive. The terror in those eyes takes me back ten years. I swore to myself I'd never give her a reason to look at me like that again, but here we are. Her hands are trembling in surrender while I'm pointing a gun at her, in her own cabin. Why...why is she sneaking into the cabin when she's supposed to know I'm here?

"What. The. Fuck?" she snarls.

I move the barrel of the rifle away, aiming at the floor. A sound somewhere between a groan and a growl escapes her as she struggles to stand. *Did I shoot her and not remember? Was she hurt somehow?* I take inventory when she's standing in front of me, checking for injury. Her hoodie hangs loosely on her, the sleeves bunching at her wrists, too long for her short arms. Black leggings hug every single curve and dip of her legs, drawing my eyes straight down to the bright pink running shoes on her feet.

There's no blood or wounds that I can see, and while I want to sigh in relief, I'm too aware of how close I came to shooting her. I can't believe I aimed a gun at Leni. Mercer's little sister, baby girl of the entire Kane family.

My Leni.

I could have shot her.

With that thought, I drop the rifle, stumbling back. Leni tilts her head, her lips moving, but I can't hear anything other than the word *shot,* ricocheting through my brain like a fucking pinball. I'm no longer in the cabin. Even though I can see her, her words don't reach me. Instead, my heart hammers out a steady beat to a volley of gunshots and mortar rounds, to shouts of 'Grenade!' and 'Medic!' I glance down at my hands; they're red, covered in the blood of a fallen Marine, and I can't breathe.

My chest tightens, black creeping at the edges of my vision, every inhale a struggle. It's been years since I've had an attack this bad. I've gone through extensive therapy, done the hard work to get myself out of the dark, and back into something resembling a real, living human again. This isn't supposed to be happening, especially not in front of Leni.

I claw at my shirt, desperate to rip the fabric off, as if that might help me breathe. I watch from a distance, detached, while Leni kneels in front of me. She touches my face, and my hands itch to defend myself from a threat that isn't real. I will not hurt her, no matter how fucked up my brain is right now.

I will not hurt Leni. Not again.

Her lips are moving, but I still can't hear anything past the sounds of gunfire and explosions. I flinch as a mortar round lands too close to us.

Clay. Her lips make the shape of my name, repeatedly, but I can't break through, can't claw my way to the surface to reach her. I want to yell at her to go, will myself to fucking pass out, and be done with this whole thing. I don't want to see her look at me with pity and concern, or worse, fear. She's looked at me with fear in her eyes before. I thought it would destroy me; part of me died *that* day.

I should've known Eleanor Kane doesn't scare easily. She proved that ten years ago, showing up on my doorstep, willing to lose herself to fix me. I should've expected that same look of sheer determination now, as her eyes dart around, searching for a solution. I feel as lost as she looks; none of my usual panic attack exercises come to mind. Maybe the lack of sleep is catching up to me. I should've taken the damn sleeping pills Doc prescribed. This is *exactly* what I want to avoid.

Clay. Those pretty, pink lips, mouth once more. Something like hesitation sparks to life in her deep green eyes. I try to look away, shame gnawing at me, my lungs tightening. She doesn't let me. Soft fingers guide my face back to hers as she leans forward and crashes her lips against mine.

The moment her lips touch mine, it's like someone hit pause, and I remember how to breathe again.

There's no more gunshots, no more screaming; only ragged breathing and jittery hands as the adrenaline seeps out of my body. I reach for her, needing something solid, something real to hold onto, careful not to grip too tight. I'm desperate to make sure she's actually there, kissing me. Her scent of lilacs and vanilla wafts from her undone hair into my nose. A scent so familiar and nostalgic that my chest starts to hurt for a different reason.

Wrapping my arms around her, I haul her into me, crushing her body against my chest, kissing her back. She tenses, muscles locking up beneath my hands. Pain slices through my lip as she sinks her teeth in. It's not a love bite, but a warning. I jerk back, slamming my head into the wall as she scrambles off me. Her chest rises and falls with each ragged breath she takes. Her hands shake, and when she manages to open her eyes to look at me, I gasp. She's angry. Livid. I think I could count on one hand the amount of times I've seen Leni this angry.

The taste of iron fills my mouth, the sting barely enough to rein me in. Leni Kane was in my lap, kissing me. I'm really fucking trying to remind myself why I can't go there with her, but it's so damn hard. Breathing the same air, staring at that gorgeous face. I realize how badly I still want her, even with that scowl.

"What the fuck are you doing in my cabin, Clay?"

I barely suppress the shudder that threatens to overtake me when she says my name. It's been too long since I've seen her. Too long since I've heard her voice, even if my name is dripping with venom when she says it. After a decade of doing my best to avoid her, I deserve that.

"Your parents have those corporate retreat things going on, and I felt like I was getting in the way. Mercer told me he asked you. He said you weren't coming back for the summer, so I've been staying here the past couple of months."

"Oh." Her eyes dart toward the door, then back to me. Fear and uncertainty fill them. That fear shouldn't be there, and knowing I caused it makes me sick to my stomach.

"I thought you knew." Scrubbing both hands down my face, I try to rein in the emotions I have flooding in and out of my system. "I, uh, I'll head over to Merc's. Come back for my stuff in the morning."

"No!" she says.

I crook an eyebrow at her, wondering, for the first time, what the hell she's doing here in the middle of the night.

"No, sorry...*fuck*." She draws her knees up into her chest, pulling her sleeves down and around her thumbs the way she used to when she was younger. "I don't want them to know I'm here."

"They're gonna know you're here, Len. That's why your dad wanted you in this cabin, so they can keep an eye on you."

"No, I know. I'm not an amateur." She rolls her eyes, huffing in frustration. *Fuck she's cute.* "I've done it before. I park in the trees, keep the lights off after dark. I just...I need a few days to regroup before they get all up in my business again."

I highly doubt they don't know when she's here. It's more believable that they realize when she sneaks back home and figures she wants to be left alone.

My fingers itch with the desire to pull her back into

me. To feel the weight of her in my arms. I'd do anything if she'd let me kiss her again, just one more time. It'll never be enough where Leni is concerned, but it would be something. The longer I hesitate, the more restless she becomes, crossing and uncrossing her arms, straightening her legs only to pull them back to her chest. Something's wrong. Something happened, and I want to fix it. Not that I have any right or that I should even be looking at her like this, but I still want to fix it. Leni in pain will never do.

Ever.

"Right, I—uh. I'll crash out on the couch until morning and go get a room from the Inn. No big deal."

She looks aghast, like I told some salacious bit of gossip. "You can't go to the inn! Then everyone will know."

"Know what, Leni?"

"Why would you leave here to stay at the inn?"

"I don't know, because you..." *Oh.* She rolls her eyes at me again, and I can't lie, the sass she's giving me is doing nothing to help the situation that has arisen in my pants. I mean, she was just sitting on me, kissing me. It's not entirely my fault.

Okay, fuck, it is my fault, and I feel like a fucking creep right now. Drawing one of my legs up, I try to hide the fact that I am sporting a semi-hard dick.

It's not solely the kiss; it's everything about her. Freckles dust her nose, which still crinkles when she's annoyed. Her hair's shorter than I remember, but it looks good. Natural waves hit right below her shoulders. I want to reach forward, run my hands through it again, wrap it around my fist while I—you know what? Nope. *Down boy.* You are not going there. Not with Leni *fucking* Kane.

The realization of what she hasn't said hits me like a

bucket of ice-cold water. Does she really think we can stay here together? "You want me to stay here with you?"

She's been back in my life for all of five minutes, and I've already had my tongue in her mouth. I have zero control when it comes to this girl. I've worked my ass off to stay away from her, so I wouldn't have to deal with this.

Eleanor is all sunshine and goodness, and she deserves someone who can reflect that back. Not someone dark and twisted like me. I won't saddle her with my mess when she has her whole life ahead of her.

"Yeah, Clay, that's the idea."

"No," I snap, the words coming out harsher than I mean. Pushing off the floor, I stomp up the stairs. I need to get my shit and get out of here before I do something even more stupid.

Something I can't take back.

www.ingramcontent.com/pod-product-compliance
Lightning Source LLC
La Vergne TN
LVHW051011080826
845145LV00009B/2567

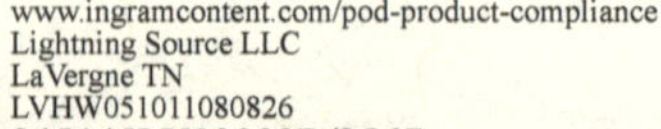

* 9 7 8 1 9 7 1 1 9 5 0 9 4 *